Mostly Magic

Short stories by

D. Gordon Hafford

Altamesa Press

Copyright © 2013 by D. Gordon Hafford

All rights reserved. No part of this book may be reproduced or transmitted in any form or by any means without permission by the author.

ACKNOWLEDGEMENT

I would like to thank all of the people who helped make this happen – first and foremost my special friend and courageous editor Anthony Bladon without whom this book would never have existed. A warm thank you goes to Paige Stone for the cover art and to Sheila Okabayashi for her graphics wizardry. Most of all I thank my family who have endured, encouraged, supported and loved me for all these years: my wonderful wife and friend of over 35 years, Deborah, and my sons David and Michael, the latter of whom is a far better author than I shall ever dream of being.

DGH

ISBN 978-0-615-81764-4

MOSTLY MAGIC

CONTENTS

FOREWORD

We all have different thresholds for surprise. For a child, it could be magical to discover a broken toy newly repaired. For a jaded adult, it might require a spaceship to land. In this collection of short stories the characters encounter a wide range of surprising scenarios. If they fail to notice small clues along the way, the outcome may seem magical. And just maybe it is.

Part 1 of this book puts everyday people in fantastic situations and explores their emotions. Fans of old school science fiction may want to turn straightaway to Part 2 of the book. If you are a child, or reading to a child, Part 3 may be the most suitable. Whatever your preference, you'll find that fortune favors the deserving, not just the crafty cats!

These stories were written purely for the enjoyment of the reader with one exception. "Is there a Santa Daddy?" is a true story and was written for my children so they could know what those last moments of wonder feel like, as they have kids of their own.

And so dear reader, dive in, enjoy and let the stories take you to places found only in dreams

PART 1

RUFFLES

Carol Masters sat in her office, feet uncharacteristically propped up on the desk, holding a computer keyboard in her lap. She gazed idly at the screen for a moment, then tapped another number into the spreadsheet she was working on. Leaning her head back, she let out a deep sigh and allowed the hint of a smile to crease her lips. Today had been a wonderful day, and tonight would be even better.

Returning her eyes to the screen she scrolled down to see the commission on the second biggest deal ever landed by the Seer Software Company. $120,503.88. Not bad for two months of hard work and a lot of anxiety. Her thoughts began to drift, as the fatigue of the last few weeks caught up with her. Certainly a new car was in order, and they did need some new furniture at home ... but what she really wanted was something else entirely. That something else was named Gordon Richards.

Looking absently at the wrinkles in the knees of her white hose, her mind flowed to thoughts of her husband Ben. They'd been together for nearly seven years now and had two kids, Billy and Kathleen. In the five years before their marriage, they'd lived together on and off but had never really been apart. In those 12 years, life with Ben had become mundane but easy. Each knew the other's weaknesses and strengths, what charged the other up and what brought the other down. But in the last year, since Ben had lost his job and now worked part-time at home, things had changed.

Never overweight, Ben had begun to lose some of his tone this last year. Meanwhile Carol had started at a health spa and her body was now tight and slim. At 5'8" with blonde hair and pale blue eyes, she had developed a striking figure, while Ben fell into complacency. She felt it was part of his "giving up" that caused him to let himself go that way, and frequently she brought up his condition in conversation.

Her newfound success coupled with his struggles to get restarted had caused a widening rift in their relationship that neither seemed to know how to bridge. So they didn't.

Her reverie was broken by the appearance of a bald head in her office door.

"Hey kid! I just heard about the EPM deal ... nice going. Out to celebrate tonight?" At 57, Art Mulroney was the oldest salesman at Seer, and also a terrible lecher. He'd continued at the company over the last few years on the strength of his past, not really generating anything new, but freely offering his bothersome advice.

"No, prob'ly just go on over to Wilson's for a drink, then on home."

"Sounds boring to me, how 'bout I take you out for a nice ..."

"Art, listen to me," she interrupted, "No matter what happens I will never, and I repeat never, go out with you for a nice ... whatever!"

"Oooo sorry, just making a little joke, Carol. I gotta go, but really, congratulations."

"Thanks," she said curtly, dismissing him with her eyes.

She'd lied to Art of course, and now she stood and smoothed her wool dress down over he knees and pushed her hair back from her face. Time to go to The Anchor Inn and Gordon.

Six months ago Gordon Richards had started in the technical support department of Seer as a consultant. Carol had worked with him on a small software sale that had become quite large and time-consuming. In their many hours of strategizing and planning together they'd felt a certain pull. A deep chemical attraction arose until they both found it hard to resist.

Physically Gordon was the opposite of Ben, tall and thin with dark curly hair and deep brown eyes that spoke to her soul. He was handsome – certainly all the women in the secretarial pool thought so – but to her it was more than looks. A kind of animal lust grew unabated until one night at The Anchor, after a particularly long planning session, they'd simply decided to get a room. It was all very matter-of-fact and, after two hours of the most passionate lovemaking of her life, she crept home, wrung out and horribly guilty.

She decided that night to cut off the affair, but the instant she saw Gordon the next day, her pangs of fidelity toward Ben evaporated. And it had happened again ... and again. The culmination of their lust had come only last weekend when Ben had taken the kids camping.

Gordon had come over Saturday afternoon, ostensibly for some work on the EPM deal. They had ended up in bed grunting and sweating until the early hours of the morning. All during the night she felt a strangeness, as if someone or something was watching, but the only one home beside herself was the cat Ruffles. Gordon thought it was quite amusing that Ruffles had watched their lovemaking from start to finish, never moving from his perch on the dresser. Carol thought it was eerie.

Hurrying across the street to The Anchor she looked briefly at her reflection in windows of the bar and straightened her hair. Inside she again had to chuckle at what she called the The Anchor's gradient. The room itself was L-shaped with tables next to windows facing the street. Another set of tables sat inside of those, then came the bar proper which was also L-shaped. The gradient was constructed of people. Near the windows, the tables held young single men and some women. Most had beer or some fashionable cocktail to drink and grasped them in their hands as if by putting them down they might lose their ability to socialize. The next set of tables, which sat in the center of each leg of the "L", were occupied mostly by secretaries and their bosses, quietly and chastely thinking of each other and getting bombed before going home to their spouse. At the bar sat the real denizens of The Anchor. They were predominantly men (any woman who sat there was presumed a hooker), each sitting hunched, talking to no one, nursing a glass of amber liquid and ice, and eking the last tendrils of smoke from a smoldering cigarette.

At the end of the bar, standing beneath a drowned out TV, his head above the hunched unidentifiables, stood Gordon. His eyes fairly sparkled as they met hers and she quickly worked her way through the close-packed tables to his side.

"So?" he said.

"All done. The deal's on Simpson's desk, all signed, filled out and ready to go. And am I ready for a drink! What're you having?" she said, leaning closer and brushing her breast deliberately against his arm.

"Scotch and water. Want some white wine? Or ..."

"Oh ... I don't know, what goes good with you?" she replied smiling and looking him in the eyes.

"With me? Oh definitely champagne. In fact that's just the thing. How about a bottle of Dom, what do you think? I bet we could get one delivered to a certain room I have reserved next door." He grinned.

"I bet we could too, but ... well let's start on it here. I'll call Berty over," she started to turn.

"No no, fair maiden, this is man's work." With that he leaned past her and signaled to the bartender who took their order with a barely concealed smirk.

Above them the TV droned on, stuck as usual on ESPN, which was showing Australian Rules football. The Dom Perignon arrived without fanfare along with two flutes standing out curiously among the squat glasses used by the others at the bar.

"Well here's ... "Gordon's toast was interrupted just as they raised their glasses by a shout from near the door.

"Hey Berty, turn on the news quick, you won't believe what's going on!" a young man blurted out.

Berty, never one to move quickly, especially when it meant upsetting his regulars at the bar, lumbered slowly to the set above Gordon and reached up to change the channel. Moments later the head of Tricia Toyota filled the screen.

"... certainly one of the most amazing, if not miraculous things in history. Our switchboards are flooded with incoming calls, and apparently all our local affiliates are besieged as well. We have reports from all over the country, which leads us to speculate that this phenomenon is at least nationwide if not worldwide. We take you now to Karen Robinson at the campus of U.C. Los Angeles where she is with Dr. Harold Pierce, head of the Animal Behavioral Studies department ... Karen?" With that the image faded to a pert young woman with her brown hair professionally atop her head and a disheveled older man in a rumpled suit whose head barely reached her shoulder.

"Dr. Pierce, as you know, sometime late last night, as near as we can figure it, domestic dogs and cats acquired the ability to speak. Can you shed some light on this incredible phenomenon for us?"

"Well, as I see it, this ability has been latent in the species for quite some time. If we look at the teachings of Darwin in this area, we see that almost any species can rise to significant levels of adaptation and evolution given the proper environment. I believe it's simply a matter of these little doggies and kitties being constantly exposed to speech and needing to communicate their needs."

"How do you explain the opinions of other prominent researchers that canine or feline speech is physically impossible?"

"Well, we can also prove that bees can't fly by the laws of aerodynamics, but as you see they do. Why should animals not talk?"

"I asked you that."

"Right."

"Well, what's the answer? Is it physically impossible or not!?" Her exasperation started to show through the thin sheen of her television persona.

"The answer is that they do, so they can, and that's it for God's sake. It's humans I wonder about."

Just as she turned to tear the puny professor into tiny academic shreds, her attention was drawn off camera and she took a deep breath and contained her anger. "This is Karen Robinson for NBC at U.C.L.A."

Tricia's face returned to the screen, but Carol's face had gone pale. The newscast continued and the entire bar now had their attention on the screen. Occasional comments drew bursts of quick laughter around them but Carol heard nothing. Her world had narrowed to a day the weekend before. A day when Ruffles had watched her and Gordon ... Oh my God, I've got to get home, she thought.

"Gordon, uh ... I've got to go. I'm sorry, maybe we can talk tomorrow okay? I've just got to go," a fine film of cold sweat coated her body now and guilt bore a hole in the pit of her stomach.

"But what about the Dom, honey? What's wrong? You can't be worried about this animal thing, can you? ... I mean ..." Gordon's thought trailed off into a silent moment. They both looked at each other and knew it could be over.

She rushed across the street and into the parking garage below her building. The drive home seemed to take longer than ever before despite the fact that there was no traffic and she sped most of the way. Pulling into the driveway of her home she said a silent prayer, hoping to keep the marriage to the man that she now realized meant so much to her and the happiness of her children. Locking the car she walked quickly to the door and let herself in.

She was greeted immediately by a cacophony of shouts and wildly excited young voices.

"Mommy, mommy, I'm so glad you're home ... know what?" Billy shouted, tugging at her skirt.

"Let me tell her, daddy," Kathleen complained, looking back from her stranglehold on Carol's other leg.

Ben rose from the couch and was smiling broadly at the two excited children. She could see that they had been sitting together all facing the coffee table ... all facing Ruffles the gray tabby, who now sat licking himself and watching the wild humans with cat-like disdain.

"Tell you what, pumpkin," Ben said to Kathleen, "how about if daddy tells her, okay?"

Kathleen pouted and clutched her mother closer, but Billy was already crying out defiantly, "Mommy, Ruffie can talk! He talks, mommy!"

"I wanted to tell," Kathleen shouted, "You stinker, you always get to tell ..."

"Now kids," Carol said, trying to keep her heart from pounding through her blouse, "you both go sit over there on the couch and we'll let daddy tell, okay?" She tried to dislodge the two urchins to no avail.

"It's really amazing, Carol, Ruffie just started talking at about 10 this morning. He walked up and said 'Loves Ruffie?' just like that. I couldn't believe my ears but he kept doing it all day. I mean the cat can really talk."

"Well ... uh ... just what does he say, Ben?"

"Oh it's funny that way. It seems all he can do is get his emotions across. He keeps saying things like 'Loves Ruffie?' and of course 'Ruffie loves.' Its like he's all emotion, you know? No real intelligence."

Carol's racing pulse began to slow. Maybe things would be okay. Maybe this whole thing was not so bad. She looked at the two children trying their best to contain themselves at her sides, but mostly at Ben. He looked somehow different now, somehow kinder more ... well ... more a part of her. And let's face it, she loved him. The love flooded back into her heart like a rushing tide and she moved to him, taking him in her arms, holding him like she would never let go.

"Oh Ben, I love you so," she said into his shoulder, tears forming in her eyes.

"Hey, what's all this?" he said, moving his head to look into her eyes, "I know you love me, but you don't have to get so emotional about it. Listen," he paused pushing her to arm's length, "I know this EPM deal has been really tough on you. How about if you and I go away for the weekend coming up. You know, without the K-I-D-S."

"No way, daddy, you're taking us!" Billy wailed.

She looked into the eyes of the man who loved her, and had stayed by her through every bad moment and every good moment, then turned to the kids. "Okay Ben, we'll take them too, but you and I, we have some catching up to do," she winked at him and smiled.

Suddenly the weight of the day and its emotional roller-coaster caught up with her and she felt hugely tired.

"I'm going into the bedroom to change, then we'll see about this talking cat," she said looking down at Ruffles who had moved over to join the group, rubbing against their legs and purring.

"Loves Ruffie?" his tiny, childlike voice asked.

She reached down and scratched the cat behind his ears where she knew he liked it the best and said "Loves Ruffie."

She turned and headed down the hall towards the master bedroom, entered it and fell backward, exhausted onto the bed. She closed her eyes for a moment and let out a deep sigh. Everything was going to be alright after all, she thought, but some strange niggling fear brushed at the back of her mind. As if she was being watched. She opened her eyes and saw Ruffles jump up onto the bed next to her and begin preening. She closed her eyes again and let her head fall back, but still that weird feeling persisted. What was wrong?

Looking up again at the cat she raised herself onto her elbows. Ruffles looked back at her steadily now, his pupils contracted to cunning slits, his eyes uncannily full of intelligence.

"Loves Ruffie?" he asked, tilting his head slightly.

She smiled and reached out to scratch him but Ruffles moved out of her reach.

"Loves Ruffie?" he repeated.

"Yes, mommy loves Ruffie," she sighed, still entranced by the cat.

Ruffles' eyes narrowed, he glanced once warily at the door, then said "How much?"

HEIRLOOM

It was early October. Eleanor and I were driving down Route 73 to my grandfather's house. It was a melancholy day, buried under the grey sky of New England. We traveled silently, both of us watching the passing skeletal remains of the elms, silhouetted against the undersides of low clouds. There were still some leaves, turned grey by the dim morning light, clinging bravely to brittle stems. I caught a glimpse of Eleanor, unconsciously pulling her lower lip with her teeth. Nervous, I thought; terrified I knew.

"You know we have to do this, Eleanor," I said to break the silence.

"I guess."

"He's eighty-five years old. He can't just live out there all by himself."

"Let's just get this over with."

"Okay, we pick him up, we take him to the rest home, we're back home ... tops, five hours. We'll be back in time for Saturday Night Live," I said, looking away from the passing pavement to her solemn face. She would not look at me.

The driveway was, like all the others, marked only by a simple mailbox perched precariously atop a small fence post. The box stared at us as we approached, its mouth agape, long since bent and corroded beyond closing. The pavement gave way to dirt as we turned up the leaf-strewn drive. I grimaced as the underside of my Honda scraped against the raised center of the dirt path.

The ancient two-story colonial seemed to follow us, moving through the trees as we drove up the tree-lined drive. After interminable minutes it finally appeared, miraculously stationary, as we cleared the last of the trees. The front of the withered building looked unnatural against the colorless sky – the lifeless hulk of what was once a home.

I looked over at Eleanor as she stared out at the house. She spoke to the window: "I won't go in. I came, but I just can't ..." She turned and looked at me with anxious eyes, then returned her gaze to the house. "You go, I'll wait here."

"Now, Eleanor," I started to say; she whirled to face me again, reluctantly giving up her vigil.

"Bill, I just can't, not with him. He scares the shit out of me, and that house ... God!"

"Listen, Eleanor, just for a minute, that's all. He's dying, I have to do what I can. He's my grandfather for God's sake," I said, as frightened as she was.

She turned back to the window and said quietly, "No Bill, you go alone. I can't go in. Just look at that place; no paint, the wood's all grey, the shutters half on, half off, uh uh, no way I'm going in there." She shivered and hugged herself.

I stared past her to the house, certain that he was watching from his study window, then turned and opened my door. No point in holding out any longer, and just driving off was out of the question now. I could not even muster a baleful glare for Eleanor as I walked around the front of the car. She sat unmoving; watching the house, as it watched us.

I mounted the rotting wooden steps and onto the portico. What had once been a proud front porch now slouched in front of the house as if one sudden pull could tear it loose. Its roof was angled to one side and had begun to separate from the house itself. Where the two pulled apart, I could see rusted nails trying in vain to stem the inevitable fall of the structure. The entire porch creaked and shifted under my weight as I stepped toward the huge oak door.

I pulled on the iron knocker and banged it feebly against the door, flakes of rust covering my fingers where I held it. No answer.

"Grampa, it's me, Bill, open the door will ya?" I looked down at my feet, not wanting to encounter the cataract-covered eye staring through the peephole. No answer.

"Come on Grampa, open the door, I can't stand out here all day." Though I could not bear to look at it, I knew the wedge-shaped peephole remained closed. If he had looked out, surely his peering eye would have bored a hole in my scalp.

"Jeez," I muttered and looked back at Eleanor as she sat dolefully in the car.

"I'm coming in whether you open the door for me or not Grampa, so come on, open up here." I banged on the knocker again. No answer.

Frustrated and slowly losing my nerve, I grabbed the door handle and pulled it down. It gave without protest, and the door swung open on groaning hinges. Had he known I was coming?

I stopped before entering and called out to Eleanor, "No answer, I'm going on in ... see you in a minute." She did nothing to acknowledge, silently regarding me with an unblinking stare.

I waved and stepped inside. It was dark. I could barely make out the pattern of a fading Persian rug covering the hardwood floor. To my right the staircase lead up to the bedrooms, its hand-rail covered with a deep film of dust. I looked up to the dim pool of blackness above; no, he had no reason to climb those steps. Only memories lie in wait up there.

I shook my head, trying to clear the cobwebs of the past, and looking around I began to remember the layout of the old place. I had come here as a child and played among the nooks and crannies of what had seemed like a great playground of a house. It beckoned to a young mind full of ghosts and fairy tales, with its secret corners and narrow closets.

Down the hall and to the left would be the kitchen. I winced imagining what must be rotting in the place where Gramma had once made cookies and cakes for me. "Big Billy; ghost hunter" my grandmother called me. I remembered her laughter filling the house as she called me in to where the goodies lay, steaming on the green tile counter. The pots and pans hanging from the ceiling surrounding the butcher block would be covered with dust now. Frozen in place by the dead air, they were copper kettle sentries guarding the door to the basement below. I would not go in there.

To my immediate right I could see into the large main room of the house. Shadows hung in the corners, waiting for their chance to grow into the dying light. The furniture was as I remembered it, though faded and grey. Large chairs huddled around a fireplace at the end of the room, where I had sat and listened to Grampa's endless stories of spirits and poltergeists.

"Off to bed young man, before these stories get your goat!" he would say lunging at me. Then he would chase me as I screamed gleefully and ran up the stairs to my room above.

Finally I looked to the left and saw the study door. He would be in there, waiting. No longer the grinning story-teller; he was a different creature altogether now. I stood for a moment at the threshold of the study, looking at my feet and wondering how hard it would be to walk back out the front door and drive back to my warm home in Boston. Not as hard as opening this door. I took a deep breath and pushed the sliding study door aside.

The gloomy interior of the study reached out for me and I felt the horror of that day flooding back into my mind. When I saw the back of his overstuffed chair, I could no longer hold off those loathsome memories.

Suddenly I was 11 years old again and standing at that study door looking at the back of that same red leather monster. My parents had left me there for the weekend, going off to New York for some shopping; dumping the kid with the grandparents. I remembered the feeling I got from Grampa the moment he met me at the door. Something had been terribly wrong in that house.

"Are those ginger cookies ready Grampa? I sure am hungry." I looked around, feeling the silence where a cheer should have been. Where's Gramma? In the kitchen?"

He looked at me absently then shambled off toward the chair. I followed, a bit perplexed.

"Hey, where's Gramma? She out shopping or something?"

He sat down heavily, breathing a deep sigh and stared out the window into the yard. I watched his chest slowly rising and falling, my youthful imagination astir. Why didn't he speak?

Finally he turned. "Gone, Billy, she's just gone right now," he croaked, his eyes looking right through me.

"Where? The store? She getting me a present?" I asked hopefully.

"Just gone," he said, looking out the window once more.

"Okay Grampa," I said and turned on my heel and left the study.

I don't like that study much, I thought; too many books. I walked around the house for a while, getting the lay of the land back in my head and planning my next ghost hunting adventure. I searched the kitchen for the goodies I knew were hiding somewhere but found nothing. Things looked unused, too clean, and Gramma was never too clean. A doubt awoke faintly in the back of my mind.

I resigned to start my ghost hunt in the basement; best place for ghosts, I figured. I went to the door at the back of the kitchen and flipped the light switch on, then opened the door. I never opened that door without turning the switch on. Never. As brave as I was at 11, I was not that brave. I opened the door, cool air hitting me in the face as I looked down into utter darkness. A chill crept up my spine like nothing I had ever felt before.

I closed the door and turned to go get my grandfather, hoping to coax him into changing the burned-out bulb. I started toward the study and stopped. Eleven years old, I thought, and not brave enough to change a bulb in a stupid old basement?! I gathered up my courage and started looking around for the bulbs. The pantry lay just off the kitchen and I found the bulbs there, in a yellow GE box laying next to a can of Calumet baking soda. I took one gingerly out of the box and carefully placed the box back next to the Red Indian on the Calumet.

I strode with false courage to the door and opened it again. I waited for a few moments, blinking, trying to get my eyes to adjust before I descended into the darkness. Grabbing the rough wooden rail, I made my way cautiously down the stairs. All the way down, I stared wide eyed into the gloom, knowing something terrible would rush out at me at any moment. Upon reaching the bottom of the stairs, I felt along the wall until I reached Grampa's work bench. I knew the light fixture hung just above the bench and by crawling onto it I would be able to reach the socket.

I kept glancing back, my eyes slowly adjusting to show the dim shapes of what were surely monsters lurking in the corners. I scrambled up onto the surface of the bench, knocking over a jar of nails in the process and got to my feet as I heard them spill onto the cement floor. I stood for a moment listening for Grampa and watching for his outline at the door; but no sound came from above. I turned and groped around in the dark, trying to make contact with the metal shade of the lamp. It found me; hitting me square in the forehead and making me just about jump out of my overalls.

I got the bulb into the socket and screwed it in. I had forgotten that the switch was left on. It burst to life, momentarily blinding me in the process. Sliding carefully off the bench, I wiped my watering eyes with the sleeve of my flannel shirt. Blinking the tears away, I surveyed the room.

This was the most wonderful part of the old house as far as I was concerned. Not only was it filled with the castaway artifacts of three generations of our family, but in the corner was one of the best things ever invented for the entertainment of young boys: a coal chute.

My eyes never left that chute as I stooped to pick up the spilled nails. I was wearing my new coveralls and my best tennis shoes but that huge pile of coal beckoned irresistibly. No mere dirt would deter me today. Hurriedly, I scooped up the last of the errant nails and placed them back in the jar, there was no question what I would do. I ran up the stairs, my small legs taking two at a time, and pounded down the hallway to the study.

"Grampa," I panted," Can I go down the chute? I mean, I brought some other clothes, and we could wash these. Is it okay Grampa, just once maybe?"

He hadn't moved from where I had left him and he did not answer me nor even acknowledge my presence. He simply stared out the window.

"Is it okay?" I asked, getting impatient.

He moved his hand as if to brush off the arm of the chair. I took this for assent and scrambled out and around the back of the house, running the entire distance.

The chute was covered with a metal door and was surrounded by tall grass. I pulled the door open and looked down into the waiting pile of coal below. I could hardly contain myself. Holding the door open, I slipped my legs over the lip of the chute, until I was sitting facing the house and holding the door up over my head. All it would take now was one quick move and I would be sliding down into the bed of wonderful sooty coal! I was filled with delicious anticipation, but somewhere from deep inside a lump built in my throat. For some reason this time was different. Staring down the chute into the darkness, my heart began to flutter and my breath came in short gasps.

This was the tricky part, and I had banged my head more than once making the entry into that chute. I was an expert now, I told myself, and there was certainly no reason for an almost fully grown boy to be afraid. This was the door to the chute, not the gaping maw of some monster waiting to swallow a young boy. I made my move and slid successfully into the hole.

The ride was over almost as it started and I landed on my backside with a satisfying crunch. I rolled over onto my stomach to slide down off the pile figuring if one plunge was good, another would be better. Just as that eerie feeling of dread had faded, something in the coal caught my eye and brought it back full force. I brushed some of the loose chunks aside to see the shiny object that I had glimpsed. Suddenly I realized what it was. Tears started to well and the cold grip of fear clutched my chest. I pushed the coal away frantically, trying desperately to deny what I saw. Eventually I was actually touching it, smearing soot all over her face and into my grandmother's dead, staring eyes.

I screamed and flailed until I reached the ground, then started backing up furiously, certain that the dead thing in the coal was not my grandmother but some zombie that would rise up to engulf me at any moment. I started to bawl and I clawed my way up the stairs again, heedless of the grime covering my body, and ran down to the study. As I rounded the corner and came into the room it hit me. This macabre discovery together with Grampa's weirdly detached behavior. He had killed her.

I stopped dead in my tracks just inside the study, more terrified now than ever before in my short life, staring at that hulking monster of a chair. I could not move, nor make a sound, I just stood whimpering and gasping for breath amid air suddenly gone stale. And then he turned. Slowly, his head came around and those terrible eyes came up to meet mine from around the chair. His gaze shot through me like an arrow. I screamed and broke for the door, running outside into a day suddenly gone cold, running for my very life. I only knew I had to get down the road away from that awful house.

Eleanor stood behind me shaking me. "Bill! Jesus, are you alright, you're scaring me to death!"

The memory must have caused me to let out another scream for now I stood, shivering in the study, with only Eleanor to support me.

"I'm okay now Eleanor," I lied, patting her hand where she gripped my arm.

She released me and started to back up toward the door; escape. I turned to her. "Just go back to the car, I'm okay," I said, trying to control my racing pulse.

"You were screaming, I mean ... I didn't know what to do. I found you standing here, in a trance or something ... Jesus." She shuddered.

"Just a minute more, I'll be out," I said. She just stood, her eyes darting between me and the chair beyond. "Go on," I prompted.

Finally she backed out of the room and I heard the porch groan at her departure. My shoulders slumped and I turned again to face that crouching chair. My heart hammered against my chest. Breath fluttered in short gasps and I fought to free my feet, to move toward the chair. As I approached I could feel the antique tomes engulfing me slowly as the room shrank to one bitter focused spot. I could see his clawed hand now, gripping the arm of the chair. I watched it, waiting for the flex of life. Any moment I would see his rheumy eyes come around the chair-back and I knew it would freeze my blood. Somehow I moved forward.

This time the hand did not move, and no stare pierced me from around the side of the chair. I took one step forward, then another and finally found myself standing next to him, still sitting in his study chair, looking only old now. And most certainly dead.

EISENHOWERS

When I sing in my car I sound exactly like Bruce Springsteen. No shit! Exactly like 'im. "I'm drivin' in my car dadada dum I turn on the radio dadada dum." See! Now I pay attention, mind you. You have to when you drive the streets of L.A. So it wasn't that I was distracted when I first saw him. It was real, man!

Three hours ago I was sitting in traffic on Sepulveda, just east of Big Santa Monica. I'm just sittin' there right, minding my own business – "Romeo and Juliet, dadada dum Samson and Delilah" – when I see him. Right fucking next to me; Dwight D. Eisenhower. I swear to God! So I'm staring at him, right? Like this guy's supposed to be dead and I'm lookin' right at him. Now I know what Ike looks like, I mean I have to be his biggest fan, but I'm mystified. This can't be Ike. This is 1988 for God's sake. So I reach over to the glove box and take out my pocket size "I like Ike" big-note songbook and check the picture on the cover. It's him!

Finally he notices me going nuts in the car next to him and he smiles at me. I'm leaning over trying to roll the window down, when I remember I have the one and only window handle on my side. By the time I've got the window down, the light's turned and half of L.A. is honking at me! Even the Orientals are honking! I flip 'em all the bird and punch the drive button on my '68 Dart. I won't buy a car unless it has buttons instead of a handle to shift with.

I can just see the rear of the Mercedes he was driving up ahead among the other cars. I've got to catch him ... it's Ike! Sweat starts to pour down my face in rivers but I don't care, or even wipe it away. I'm hot on the trail of the General himself. I'm swerving in and out trying to get an advantage, but as usual, whatever lane I'm in is the slow one. I can see Ike getting away but I have an opening on the right of another car as I approach Pico. I make my break at the same time as a little Datsun pulls out of a space but I catch him just on the front fender. That awful crunch!

So for the moment I've forgotten about Ike and I'm thinking; late for work, no insurance ... not again! I get out and walk around my car to check out the damage. No problem for the old Dart, I mean this car is built! The bumper's not even scratched ... but the Datsun ... accordion time. I'm bending over taking in this guy's crumpled fender when I look up to see him leaning over from between the cars. It's Ike! My brain does a double flip. How can this be Ike? I just lost Ike in his Mercedes which must be 10 blocks away by now. I stand to get a better look and sure as shit it's Ike! I start to blubber, "Jeez Ike, I'm sorry about the car, but hey man, I'm your biggest fan! I've got all the campaign stickers the buttons ... everything!"

He doesn't say a word. He just looks real surprised, like "What's wrong with this moron?" then starts to back away. I climb up over my hood with my hand out, "Come on Dwight ... uh, can I call you Dwight? No matter, Mr. Eisenhower, will ya shake my hand? Please will ya?"

He's still backing away and now he looks as scared as a cat in lane two of the 405. I can't figure this out. If he's some kind of Hollywood Ike look-alike then he should just say so, but this guy don't make a sound. Finally, he gets in his car and rolls up the window. I'm staring in at the guy, both hands on his window. "Hey man, I hit your car, don't you want my license number or something?"

He's shaking his head and he starts the car! I can't believe this, the guy's car is toast and he's gonna drive away! But he can't 'cause I got him trapped against the curb with my car. Now he's realized he's trapped and he's completely terrified. So I figure, I got to settle down or there's gonna be trouble.

No sooner than I think it, along comes trouble in full black and white. No less than two of L.A.'s finest out to spoil my day. And I saw Ike and everything!

The first cop comes up while the other gets on the radio. "What seems to be the trouble here?" he asks. I mean if I ran over a guy, then left him under the car, the cops would still say, "What seems to be the trouble here?" They must learn that in cop school. Just when I'm about to answer, up comes the other cop. Another Ike! This is getting ridiculous. I'm looking back and forth between the guy in the car and the second cop and they're both Eisenhowers! Now I know something's messed up.

"Come on son, out with it," the non-Ike cop says. Another cop school standard; everyone is either their son, their pop, or Ma'am. Why do they think we're all related to them? I'm still a bit small even at thirty, so that puts me in with the "sons." Anyway, the only thing I can spit out is "Ike."

I know it comes out like a squeak more than a name but I just can't make words while there are two Ike's within spittin' distance. This is awesome! But I gotta say something or they're going to haul me away to the nut house. I've been there once man, that's enough. Just make a sound, I tell myself, and it'll turn into words.

"Ike, uh, hey man, this guy in the Datsun looks like Dwight D. Eisenhower ... and so does your partner ... Dad," I sputter. I spit a little when I talk, so he has to wipe his face.

"I'll ignore the Dwight D. Eisenhower part, and by the way it's a Toyota son ... Now did you hit this man's car?" he says, backing out of my range.

I wanted to say "No, this Mazda has just got that new custom accordion look and I was comparing the finish," but all that comes out is "Yeah, but ... "

"Okay, that's step one. Just calm down and let the nice man out of his car please."

"Alright officer, but if it is Ike will you make him sign my big note song book, I got it right here in the ..."

"Son, you're gonna have to settle down. Just stand away from the car and put your hands on the top okay, both hands."

"I will, but hey!"

Suddenly he grabs me, pushes my feet apart and twists my arm behind my back! Christ that hurts! On goes the first cuff and he's going for my other arm. Now I've watched All Star Wrestling and MacGyver and I know every hold in the book. There's only one way to get out of this one; I'm goin' for an atomic pile driver on this guy!

Next thing I know I'm face down on the pavement, my head in an oily puddle. My mouth is bleeding and his foot smells terrible. I think he must have stepped in something other than my face today. I gotta work on that atomic pile driver.

Now I've got to explain before I go on, that during this whole melee, neither of the Eisenhowers has made a peep. Nothing.

So they put me in a jacket, and shove me into the patrol car like I'm some sort of loony tune. I'm tryin' to tell them, I just wanted to see Ike.

Next thing I know, I've moved into a new home. I somehow missed the trip there, but my head is exploding and I can feel some swelling near my eye. I'm in a room about eight by eight, nicely padded and boy is this place secure. You can't be too careful living in L.A. Looking up, I can see that the only light is a fluorescent, recessed into the ceiling. Man, I think, it's gonna be a bitch to change that bulb. Through the peephole in the door I see occasional faces peering in at me. "Here I am!" I shout. "Come on in, let's play some Parcheesi!" I'm feeling quite calm, and by now the fact that every fifth face is Ike – well, it doesn't bother me anymore. I've finally figured that part out. It's Hollywood; with plastic surgery these days, they can do anything. So why wouldn't every few faces look like Ike, eh?

IS THERE A SANTA, DADDY?

A little less than a year ago, my wife called me into our room and told me we had to talk. It seemed that very afternoon, our now almost eight-year-old had asked the first of many hard questions. Up until that Christmas, Santa Claus had always visited our house. His writing on the packages was always carefully disguised and his wrapping different than anything wrapped in our children's presence. He ate the cookies carefully left out for him and there was always just a tiny bit of milk left in his glass in the morning. The gifts he brought were always left near the fireplace, and not under the tree like the others. All in all, his visits were a source of great joy and excitement for our two sons for whom he was as real as sunshine and breakfast cereal. Until that day.

"He wants to ask you if there is really a Santa Claus. He's a little upset and I told him he'd have to talk to you." She paused, "So?"

"So?" I answered, looking directly at her.

"What are you going to tell him?"

I held her eyes with mine; "I'm going to tell him that there absolutely, without a doubt, is a Santa Claus."

She stared at me for a moment and then smiled. After twenty years, she already knew the answer to her question. "Okay," she said, "Just be careful what you say, alright?"

While she went in the other room to get him, I began to think about what she'd said. Depending on what and even how I answered him, there might be effects beyond our home. Other kids at school for example, who might ridicule him for thinking like his old man, or even worse, might call his father a liar. I also knew this was a test of sorts. Our son was a bright boy and he prided himself in discovering the nature of things without our help. I knew that he had already figured out the Santa answer, but was looking at us – me really, to see what we'd say. So this was not only the time when every parent has to reveal the Santa Claus myth to his or her child, but it was something more. A question of whether we would lie to him about something. Somewhere inside me a small part also thought about another little boy, over 30 years before, looking quietly out his window and wondering if magic really existed in the world. In the end, I had only a moment to decide on what I'd say, and though I'd been thinking about this moment for years, I suddenly doubted I could go through with it and really tell him the truth. My hesitation lasted scarcely a second though. It would have to be the truth or I wouldn't pass the test. The path was clear. I only hoped I could make him understand and suddenly I knew how. I decided to let that little boy, who still lives inside me, tell my son about Santa Claus.

Our son came into the room and assumed a posture of "I'm a smart kid so don't even try to lie to me." Without saying a word, he simply stared at the floor and I knew right then that his mind was made up. There was nothing left but the test itself.

"Mommy tells me you are wondering about Santa Claus. Is there really a Santa Claus or not; is that right?"

"Daddy!" He rolled his eyes. Of course there was no Santa, how stupid could I be?

"I know what you are thinking," I said, "but you are wrong. You're thinking, how can this fat old elf come down our chimney and leave these presents that were clearly bought at Toys"R"Us? You're thinking, how can one, admittedly magical, character possibly visit every kid in every town throughout the world in a single night? Not possible, is it? No, of course not, and I wouldn't expect you to believe that anyway. But there most definitely is a Santa Claus and I know it as sure as I know you and Mommy and your little brother. So I'm going to tell you how I know and then you can decide for yourself what you believe ... that okay with you?"

He nodded, listening now, his attention clearly held, but wary.

"When my Dad – your Grandfather – and my Mom, who you never knew, first got married, they had no money at all. It was all they could do to make ends meet, buy food, and pay the rent and such. As Christmas approached, they vowed that neither would buy a gift for the other, thus saving the last $20 or $30 they had for necessities. When Christmas morning came, not only had he bought her a gift, but she'd bought one for him as well. Not only that, but between the two of them, they'd somehow spent more than they actually had, leaving them dead broke." I paused, trying to catch his eye.

"Well these things have a way of sorting themselves out and they didn't go hungry. In fact I can remember them telling me that story many times and how, when they'd discovered that each had broken their promise, they laughed so hard they cried."

"Daddy, what's that got to do with Santa Claus?" He looked impatient.

"Well, let me finish and I think you'll see," I smiled, trying to lighten his mood.

"When I was about 10 years old, I lived in a neighborhood full of other boys, all at least one year older than I was. The Christmas before, my parents had stored a matching pair of bicycles in our garage destined for two of my friends. They were shining silver Stingrays, indisputably the best bike ever made for a kid. I was, of course, too young for such a bike because the handlebars were much too high for me to reach and be safe. At least that's what my parents told me. To say that I was jealous would have been a massive understatement. As a new Christmas approached we received a gigantic catalog from Sears, filled with every imaginable 'gift idea.' Each page was covered with bright colors and wide-eyed children and adults receiving the gifts of their dreams. I found mine on page 528. It was the most beautiful thing I'd ever seen in my life. It was of course a Stingray. Maroon, with a 5-speed shifter and stretched frame; this was not a bike, but a work of art. To this day I remember running in to find my Dad, laying the catalog in front of him and pointing. 'I want that!' I announced.

"He looked at the picture, then at the price tag and finally at me. He didn't say anything at the time, just listened to me oohing, aahing and making my case for my ability to tame the butterfly handlebars and banana seat.

"I took that catalog into my room and put it in my dresser drawer, right next to my bed. Every night, and I mean every night, I opened up that catalog, which was by then dog eared and fell open automatically to page 528, a.k.a. the bike, and simply stared.

"One night my parents both came into my room and sat me down to talk. 'Listen honey,' my Dad began, 'I know you want that bike in the Sears catalog, but we just can't this year. That bike is over $75 and we simply can't afford it. We wanted to tell you now so you wouldn't get your heart set on it.'

"I was crestfallen. 'I understand,' I told them, and even though I was holding a torrent of tears inside, I tried to be stoic. I doubt it worked, but they seemed to appreciate the try.

"That night, I opened the drawer again and looked at the bike. It was still beautiful and I thought, maybe next year.

"When Christmas morning came, I awoke early, just like you guys do, and went to wake my parents. In our house, you didn't go out into the living room where the tree was until Mom and Dad came with you, just like we make you kids wait. I think now about that house and what I remember most clearly, is the hallway. As you emerged from the hall, the living room was on your left and I remember it for one simple reason. That morning, when I made that turn, the thing I wanted most in the world was waiting for me under our tree. The bike stood, on its kickstand, waiting for the boy who'd loved it best, the morning sun shining brightly off the chrome and maroon metal flake paint. I will never forget that moment. I turned to my parents, bursting with joy. They simply shrugged and said, 'Santa must have brought it, Dougie ... Merry Christmas.'

"Now, since I was well past believing in Santa Claus, I knew they'd gotten me the bike, but something strange happened to me that morning. I suddenly realized that it really was Santa Claus who'd gotten me the bike. That and all the wonderful gifts past and future, even the ones I myself had given with the greatest joy, all came from Santa Claus. That was 32 years ago son, and I remember it like it was yesterday."

At this point I was becoming quite emotional and so I knelt down to my son's level with tears filling my eyes.

"Santa is in here son," I said, putting my hand on his chest, "He's in your heart. He's not a person or an elf or any magical being. He's inside of you. He's the spirit of giving, the love you have for others and the special way you feel around Christmas time. Santa is that magical thing that makes a young couple spend the last of their money on each other and remember it all their lives. Santa is the guy who makes parents work things out so their son can have that maroon Stingray bicycle, even though it costs far more than they can spend. Santa Claus gives us one special time, every year, when people do extraordinary things for those they love.

"So, even now son, when your Mom asked me what I was going to tell you, I told her 'the truth', because there really is a Santa Claus."

"AND AMAZING CLOSET SPACE!"

I can remember Mr. Delvecchio showing me around the apartment like it was yesterday. Frankly, I was a little surprised at how low the rent was. Considering its location, 5th and California in Santa Monica, it should have rented for half as much again as the $1,250 per month he was asking. Not only was the building close to the beach, but it had been completely refurbished with the sole exception of one small closet in the master bedroom. In short, it was beautiful. You walked into a courtyard style entryway, filled with green broad leaf plants and illuminated by a skylight. The front door opened into a large living room, dominated by a sandy stone fireplace and mantle. Huge, black leather couches faced each other at the room's center, set off by a tan Berber carpeting that made it look about twice its 20 x 20 size. Partitioned off a by a bar was a magnificent kitchen, filled with gleaming state-of-the-art appliances, including a Viking, dual oven stove, and a Sub-Zero refrigerator that talked.

The front bedroom was rather small, but I was going to use it as an office anyway, and besides, the master bedroom was enormous and that's all I really cared about. The bed was king-size, contained in a shining chrome frame and covered by a patchwork quilt. And of course there were plenty of mirrors all around. I love mirrors; I'll let you guess why. The only odd thing in the entire apartment was a tiny closet located in the master bedroom. It was situated in an unusual location, in the middle of a wall, directly across from the foot of the bed. Access was through a small set wooden of doors, apparently still there from the original builder. The doors could only be described as dingy. The aged, unidentifiable wood was dark brown and in the exact center, were two of the strangest crystal knobs I had ever seen. I guess I just figured what the hell, I can always have the doors redone and get rid of those ugly knobs. So I didn't think much about it. At $1,250 per month, I just said, "Delvecchio my man, I'll take it, let's do forms!"

And so we did.

I moved in the following weekend, on July 14th, the night I met Mary. I'll never forget her because she was the first. I'd gone to the King's Head for a couple of Guinness and was sitting at the corner of the bar, thinking how nice it was to be within walking distance of my favorite English pub. Looking up, I noticed her walking towards me; all red miniskirt and black stockings. I guess that's all I saw, because as I recall, her face ... well, I'll get to that.

"I've been watching you from across the room," she said, showing bad teeth between unusually red lips. "You look extremely interested in that pint. Care for some conversation?"

So I'm male and single and I said, "Sure, have a seat."

Next thing I know, it's midnight, several Guinness later, she's looking much better, and we're wobbling toward my place on foot. We arrived, only partially sobered by the walk, about 15 minutes later. Five minutes after that we were entangled in a sweaty heap on the bed. I was in rare form that night, or should I say forms – plural! Anyway, I remember collapsing at about two or 2:30 in the morning unable to regain ... oh well, you get the picture. It could not have been much later than that, when I first heard the voice.

"Hey," it said, "wake up!"

I looked over at Mary (at least I think that was her name ... I'm pretty sure) who lay on her back, gasping great gulps of air between snores.

"Hey! You! Over here. Don't look at her, dipshit; over here!" The voice became more emphatic.

That's when I realized where it was coming from. The closet. Now I can tell you that I felt pretty stupid at that particular moment. I couldn't very well answer a closet, and I was lying in bed next to a woman that was not only beginning to look substantially different than what I remembered from the bar but snoring like a 747 preparing for takeoff. I just stared at the two wooden doors and tried desperately to tell myself that this could not be happening.

"Look! I'm over here! Are you deaf?"

"No," I said quietly, looking askance at my companion.

"Then answer me when I talk to you, for God's sake. Now listen pal ... by the way, what's your name?"

"Bud," I answered, suddenly sober and wondering just what the hell was going on.

"Okay, Bud. Shit, what a stupid name; Bud. You must work at a gas station with a name like that – somewhere where you have to wear a shirt with your name on it. Bud! Shit ..."

"No, I'm an accountant with ..."

"Oh shut the fuck up, Bud. Listen, who gives a damn about your name anyway; I'm hungry. How 'bout throwing Old Closet a little something to eat, eh?"

Now I was becoming intrigued. Even considering the immense pressure building behind my forehead, this Stephen King moment was really getting to be interesting.

"And what would Mr. Closet like to eat?" I asked, playing along with my own hallucination.

"*She* would do nicely I think. I do like them on the plump side of course, but she'll do."

"Oh she would, would she? And just how do I feed her to you? Shoes first, then hang her up?"

"Oh funnnnneee Bud, real 'A' material."

"Well, I'm most certainly not going to feed you my ... uh ... guest. Is there anything else you'd like to eat?"

"I suppose I could eat you. But then it'd be a while before some other poor schmuck moved in. And I'd just be back in the same boat. So I guess the answer is no. I want her. And make it snappy, it's been a while."

"This is all a bad dream I'm having, Closet. You are just a figment of my imagination," I said confidently, doubting all the way. I continued,

"So ... I'm going back to sleep and in the morning, over breakfast, she and I will just laugh at all this."

"Okay Bud. Have it your way. But just remember, I'm here for you ... you know... if you change your mind or something." The closet was silent from then on, and eventually, I drifted off.

I awoke the next morning with the sun streaming through my blinds and showing Mary's face in full light. "Hi lover," she said, reaching out to stroke my leg.

I jumped back, unable to conceal my revulsion. Oh my God, I thought I was going to be sick. Her face was half smeared makeup and half ash gray elephant hide, surrounding dull brown eyes. Her thin lips, disguised by cakes of bright red lipstick from the night before, now gave her smile a skeletal quality. I was dumbstruck. Wondering what to do and feeling that dull, alcohol spike drilling into my forehead, I faintly heard the doorbell ring. My heart did a complete flip and attempted to eject itself via my throat. I'd completely forgotten. Belinda, my fiancée was due to arrive, no doubt wearing her cutest jogging outfit and ready for our planned run up San Vicente boulevard. Oh shit.

"Who's at the door, lover? Want me to get it?" Mary said, starting to rise.

"*No!*" I fairly shouted. Then more quietly I said, "No, no, it's alright, I'll get it."

I didn't know what to do. If Belinda found me with any woman, let alone the Sea Hag here, I'd be sunk. Two years of *great*, down the tubes! My mind, still fogged and swimming in the dregs of Guinness Stout, was racing in tight circles ... what to do?

"Ahem," came a voice from across the room. "Did you say something, lover?" Mary asked, smiling.

Ugh, I thought. I had to get out of this predicament somehow. "Uh, yeah, would you mind getting my robe for me?"

"Sure lover, where is it? Down here?" she made another lunge for me.

Successfully eluding her grasp, I said, "Over there in Mr. uh ... I mean in the closet. The small one with the wooden doors."

Standing, she made what she must have thought was a flouncy turn and walked, sagging buttocks rocking to and fro, to the closet and opened the door.

"Oh, it's dark in here, is there a light?"

"Just a little further in ..." I started to say, when suddenly she was gone. Vanished in the blink of an eye. The door slammed shut, I heard it rattle two or three times, then it bulged out into the room, as if made of rubber. Finally, the door shrank back to normal, with a few bumps and rumbles, then fell into silence.

For a moment I couldn't believe it. I just sat there in bed dumbfounded. Then the door opened, just a bit, and I heard a hollow... *buurrrrp*!

The door slammed.

At that moment, the bell rang again, jolting me back to reality. I stood gingerly on shaky legs, hastily swept Mary's underwear under the bed, and wandered through the living room to the front door, giving the closet a wide berth. On the way, I grabbed a comb.

As I approached, Belinda was peeking around the edge of the door through smoked glass. "Hey, wake up, sleepy head," she said, in a muffled but cheerful voice.

Still confused, and not sure Mary was gone, I stepped cautiously up to the door and opened it, comb in hand

"Hi honey. Come on in, sit down here a minute, I was just finishing up in the bathroom," I muttered, turning my back on her and walking back toward the sanctuary of my ablutions. I figured I'd just bide my time and see what happened.

Nothing did.

We went jogging, had a nice breakfast later at Fromin's, and then went out to an afternoon movie. It was an altogether pleasant day, and by 8:00 p.m. I had forgotten all about Mary, Mr. Closet and a hangover long since past.

About two months later, I was back in the King's Head, at my usual stool, looking for action. My closet problem had turned into a blessing. He'd get hungry at about the same rate as I would get restless for a little ... adventure. You could say, we had a mutually satisfying relationship. I fed him, he kept me out of trouble with Belinda and all was well with the world. Oh, I got some guilt feelings along the way, but hey, it's kind of their fault too. I mean, picking up guys in a bar like the Head? Oh come on now. Okay, okay, so it's bullshit, but that's what I said to myself.

Then came the night that everything changed. It was late September and the evening was a bit sultry. I can remember walking home with Malika, joking about how warm it was and how warm we could make it. Malika was an exotic woman, black and possessed of deep brown almond-shaped eyes and the biggest set of Winnebagos I'd seen outside *youporn.com*. Why she'd agreed to go home with me I'll never know, because almost every guy in the place had made a run at her. Anyway, she picked me up, and there we were – singing, walking arm in arm and making lewd jokes as we walked up California towards 4th. Just as we turned into my courtyard, I spotted a little red car across the street just like Belinda's. For a moment my heart leapt into my throat, but I kept walking as if nothing happened. As I closed the door behind me, I turned surreptitiously to watch the car start up and pull away. I couldn't quite get the license number, but I decided it couldn't have been Belinda. She was supposed to be in Fresno that night on business so I shrugged it off as paranoia. My heart eventually slowed its pounding, but I couldn't quite get that red car off my mind. That is of course until Malika walked out of the bathroom nude, holding her breasts in her hands and looking at me like I was the cherry on top of a chocolate sundae.

Poor Malika. What a waste of fine womanhood. Of course, old Mr. Closet was extremely pleased. But that night I came to a decision. No more. I just couldn't do it to the women or myself, nor take any further chances with my beloved Belinda. It had to stop.

Two days later I came home to find my apartment brightly lit. A bit surprised, I opened the already unlocked door and walked inside to an incredibly set table with white tablecloth, sterling silver candlesticks and my beautiful Belinda holding a roast platter between green oven mitts.

"Thought I'd surprise you, Bud. I hope it's okay?" she said, settling the roast in amid serving dishes filled with wonderful steaming food. She stepped away from the table and came to me, removing the mitts and wrapped her arms around me.

"What a wonderful surprise." I smiled, then accepted her proffered lips. "What's the occasion?"

"Oh nothing, except well ... I've been thinking." She looked serious now, pulling back and staring me in the eye. "It must get lonely here all alone. And you must have asked me a dozen times to move in with you. So, I decided to accept. I moved in today."

"You're kidding – really? Um I uh ... "

"Oh you don't have to look so surprised. You knew I'd break down sooner or later, didn't you?"

"Well, yes. Yes, I guess I did. I'm so ... uh, happy," I said trying desperately not to show my trepidation. All I could think about was the closet.

"I sold all my furniture this weekend. I know I told you I was going to Fresno. I just wanted this to be a surprise. Anyway, I sold the stuff we wouldn't need and moved the rest in today. I just took over that one old closet your weren't using in the bedroom. I hope you don't mind?"

My stomach rolled over into a tight, cold ball. I couldn't breathe for at least 10 seconds and for a moment, I was sure I would pass out. My wonderful, beautiful, smart, laughing, I'd-give-anything-for-you, Belinda ... went in *the closet*!

"Uh ... uh... "

"You look like you just saw a ghost, Bud. What's the matter?" she asked, her face a mixture I couldn't read.

"Look, if you want me to move my stuff out I can just ..."

"No!" I croaked, "Don't. Its just ... well, I'm just so happy you're here. I was just a bit choked up that's all."

I tried to regain my composure. If she'd put her clothes in the closet then ... maybe he was gone. Could I hope? I wondered; could this have turned out so perfectly, that the thing in the closet was gone too, along with all evidence of my infidelity? "Did you really use that musty old closet?" I asked.

"Sure, come on in here, I'll show you."

"No, no, it's okay, we can't let this awesome meal get cold. After dinner, okay? Then we can talk about where your stuff goes and our plans ..." she stopped me mid-sentence with a kiss.

That night was incredible. After a spectacular dinner we made love like it was the very first time. With the stamina of teenagers and the experience of knowing each other's bodies for more than two years, it was pure ecstasy. And for the first time in my life I awoke knowing I could look to my side and see something truly special and absolutely real.

She looked up at me with sleepy eyes, blinking away the fatigue of the night.

"Mm, nice," she said, squinting at the tangled mop of my hair.

I brushed it aside and gave her a soft, lingering kiss.

"Morning."

"Yes. Morning and I'm famished. You took a lot out of me last night," she said mockingly.

"Put quite a bit *in* too as I recall," I laughed and started to get up.

"Oh don't," she said, pulling me back down to the bed, "I'll make you breakfast, how's that?"

"Fine, but I have to get up. Nature calls, you know."

"Okay, but will you hand me my robe from the closet before you go into the bathroom. It's a bit chilly."

I didn't even think. I simply went to the old wooden doors and grabbed the knob. The crystal seemed to fight my hand for a moment, then gave in. The door came open easily then and I stared into the dark, not noticing the shadow behind me.

Suddenly I felt two hands shove hard against my back, and "Time to feed Mr. Closet, Bud," were the last words I heard on mortal earth.

At first, I was really upset about all the guys she brought by. But I got over it after she finally fed me the first one. It's not like I have reason to be jealous or anything ... But it's been a while now since Belinda moved out. And lately I've been so lonely ... and so hungry.

OCARINA

For a young boy, going to a rest home to see an aging grandparent is about the nearest thing to hell imaginable. The smell of disinfectant, the staring and empty eyes scattered randomly about the hallways, and the incessant drone of televisions at full volume, make such places terrifying and confusing to the mind of a child.

For me, Grandpa and the home were one and the same. I had never known the man my mother spoke of: robust and vigorous, full of life and wisdom. He'd been a maker of fine furniture, skilled with hand tools to a degree few craftsmen are today. As I write this, I sit at a magnificent desk he made nearly 50 years before my birth. As my 50th birthday approaches and its 100th, it is still as resplendent as the day it was made.

Grandpa, to an eight-year-old boy, was just a shriveled old man who sat calmly in a chair and smiled in a hopelessly lost way when we came to visit. My mother always let me bring a favorite toy so I would not get bored while she droned on about family problems, the antics of my younger brother (who never seemed to have to endure such torture), me, and the progress of my father's business affairs. He never spoke but would listen attentively, his eyelids occasionally drooping, smiling away regardless of the good or bad of my mother's story. To say I loved him would be a lie, although my parents insisted I did. But one day all that changed, and for a moment I was to glimpse the essence of what had once been a truly remarkable man.

It is difficult to remember things much before the age of 10 years once we reach adulthood, but I was exactly eight the day we went to see

Grandpa for the very last time. For several months he'd been "quite ill" as my parents put it, hiding from us his deterioration from liver disease and congestive heart failure by means of a euphemism designed for small and simple minds. I often heard my mother sobbing late at night with my father's voice mixed in, reciting tired clichés like "It's for the best, Meg," and "He'll be in a better place when all this is through." Somehow both my brother and I had figured out that Grandpa wasn't going to be around much longer, but thoughts of Grandpa and his imminent demise seemed as distant as the sun on that particular day. It was my birthday.

That afternoon I'd left school flushed with excitement to get home and play with the new toys I'd been given earlier that morning. I remember running full tilt across the blacktop of the school yard towards my mother's station wagon, carrying in my hand a most cherished gift. It was a small, colorfully painted ocarina. My teacher, Mrs. Bobbin, who loved music and who could infuse that love in even the dullest student, had given me this special gift for my birthday. Having both a mild crush on Mrs. Bobbin and a child's wide-eyed dream of being a musician made this tiny wooden instrument a prize beyond reckoning. I stumbled as I ran and nearly fell, but fortune smiled on me and I recovered without incident and made it to the car. There were the usual greetings – a kiss for my mother and her entreaties to me to fill her ears with the routines of a child's day at school – and then the bottom fell out of an otherwise wonderful day.

"We're going to stop by and see Grandpa on the way home, Davey," she said matter-of-factly, as if this were a simple task like picking up a dozen eggs or my father's shirts at the laundry.

Mom!" I cried, "It's my birthday, I don't want to go see Grandpa today!" A tear fell down my cheek and I began the grimace that I knew would threaten her with an all-out tantrum.

"Listen, Davey, I know it's your birthday and you deserve to have a nice day, but Grandpa needs to see you today. You'll just have to do this one thing. Then the day is yours okay?"

"Today?" I spouted between fits of crying and pouting, "Why does he have to see me today?"

"Well, sweetheart, he just does, okay?" She sighed and looked at me in the plaintive way only a mother can. "It's important or I wouldn't ask you to do it. Be a big guy now and don't cry in front of Grandpa. Just let him see you this one time." She hadn't said "last" but I heard it nonetheless.

"Fine," I huffed and leaned against the window, avoiding her gaze and examining my ocarina between deep sighs and eight-year-old looks of disgust. She said no more, and simply drove us to the home.

Lakewood Manor was as aged as its constituents but still held some beauty, surrounded as it was by a luxuriant green lawn and patches of flowers that always seemed to be in bloom. We entered through a pair of glass doors and were immediately assaulted by the vile smells of urine, disinfectant and things unmentionable. The attendant at the front desk looked up at us briefly, vaguely interested, but soon moving back to the pages of the National Enquirer as we walked past. He'd seen us many times and was satisfied we knew our way.

When we reached Grandpa's room I was mildly surprised to see the bed next to his empty and freshly made. The pictures that had adorned the wall surrounding it were all gone and the dull green coverlet was all that was left as evidence of his suitemate. Grandpa was in his accustomed place, looking out the window at the garden and sunshine beyond. He looked up at us once we entered his field of view, and then drew a smile from deep in the folds of his face. My mother pulled up a chair and sat directly before him, taking his hands in hers. I remember quite clearly how he carefully looked down at where her hands held his then back up at her. It was a slow, almost painful movement but his smile endured throughout as if to say, "You're here, that's all that counts." For a moment she simply looked at him. The tears in her eyes threatened to spill over her lower eyelids at any second, but she gamely smiled and tilted her head to one side while patting his hand.

Before she could begin her habitual recitation of the events in the outside world, a well-dressed young man looking entirely out of place entered the room and walked up to my mother. "Good afternoon, Meg," he said, without the smallest glance at my Grandfather or me. "Can we speak for a moment outside?" She looked up at him and again the tears filled her eyes. Choking them back she stood and released my Grandfather's hands from hers.

"Yes, of course, let's go out in the corridor," then turning to me, "You stay here with Grandpa, Davey. Tell him all about your birthday and all the stuff you got, okay?"

That's when I lost it. "*No!*" I screamed. "I'm going with you, Mom! I don't wanna stay here!" I was doing a good job of sobbing and I leapt from the bed towards my mother, in the process dropping my precious ocarina, stepping on the delicate mouthpiece and feeling an awful crunch.

For a moment, I was simply stunned. I looked down at the instrument, wondering if I should hope for some miraculous act of God to put it back together, but as my mother stooped and picked it up, I could see my hopes would be futile. The fat center portion was intact, but where your mouth went to blow sweet notes into the end it was cracked and broken, its beautiful paint scraped away to reveal jagged edges. My mother knelt down and held it out to me, her head tilted in the same I love-you-but-I-can't-help-you way she'd looked at Grandpa. I began to sob in earnest now, unable to speak.

"We'll get you another one, Davey. I'm sure Mrs. Bobbin can tell us where she got it. We'll get another just like it, okay?" she said, trying to remain calm. I simply took the ocarina from her and held it cupped in my hands. "Listen, Davey, I really have to talk to Dr. Marks, okay, just give me a minute and I'll be back." And with that she walked outside, leaving me in tears and desperately alone.

For what seemed an eternity I simply stared down at the ruined ocarina in my hands. Then, for the first time in my life, I heard Grandpa speak.

"Davey?" It was almost a whisper. For a moment I pretended I did not hear.

"Davey?" This time I glanced up, afraid of what I might see, and there he was, looking directly at me. I'd always been repelled by Grandpa and more than a little afraid but at that moment, he seemed somehow to have transformed himself from a shriveled and frightening ghost to simply an old man. Quickly I looked back down at the broken thing in my hands.

"Can I see it Davey?" he held out his trembling, leathery hand.

I looked up at him again, seeing his eyes as if for the very first time. Deep within them I could see a sort of light that I'd never seen before and I found myself wondering if anyone else had seen that light. I passed the ocarina into his hand almost reverently and he gently clasped it then brought it to his breast holding it in both hands, obscuring it from my view.

"It's quite beautiful, Davey," he said. I could only nod, still fighting back sobs of anger and frustration. He smiled now in a mischievous way. "They think I can't talk, did you know that? I can though. Just don't want to. Got nothing to say, so all I do is listen." But with me he was talking! He leaned closer.

"Your mom ever tell you what I did for a living son?"

I nodded, still a little confused and afraid. "I used to make furniture. Nice stuff, out of wood you know. I knew the wood then quite well, quite well." He took a deep wheezing breath and I could tell this talking was taking its toll. As if his life were ebbing with each breathy whisper.

"Funny thing, Davey. I always thought there was something special about wood – having been alive and all." He took several deep breaths, holding my gaze in his. I had stopped sobbing now and was listening intently.

"I always thought that in here," he held his clasped hands to his chest, "I had one really great work inside. One that could only come from the heart." He stopped for breath again, this time more labored than before. "In all my life, that one really great piece never happened." I could see his eyes filling with tears. "I don't really know why but maybe it's 'cause you've only got one chance and God makes sure the time is right before he gives it to ya." He looked down at his hands.

"Maybe this is it," he said. "God knows it's time."

Grandpa's eyes closed, for what was to be the last time, and his hands fell open. Within, was a small, colorfully painted ocarina, completely whole.

HEADHUNTER

Good afternoon Mr. Ozawa. Did I say that right?"

"Yes, perfectly. Thank you for seeing me."

"My pleasure entirely, Mr. Ozawa. Excuse me, but may I call you Daniel?"

"Of course, please do. Your offices here are very nice. The placement business must be doing well?"

"Well, you know, the economy isn't what it used to be and we've had our struggles. But, by branching out into other areas and seeing, well, people like yourself, we've been able to do quite nicely."

"I am most pleased to hear that, Ms. Goldberg."

"Yes, well Mr. uh ... Daniel, let's get to work here. The first thing we'll need, before we can find you the right position, is some background to fill out this resumé."

"Certainly."

"What I'd like to do is go over it in detail with you, perhaps make some suggestions about wording, presentation and such and get a fuller picture of your employment history."

"Excellent."

"Well Daniel, first you've listed a few jobs at fast food restaurants and the like. I think we should remove them. Do you agree?"

"Whatever you think is best."

"That will leave us with a more concise, focused package. It says here that you were trained at an academy at a secret island location. Can you tell me more about that?"

"Well, it was your basic ninja school. We did various group exercises and practiced things like hitting each other with these little sticks attached to a chain, and sneaking around in these really cute skin-tight black outfits."

"Um hmm ... and did you receive any sort of degree or certification? I don't see anything listed."

"No, this secret agent fellow swooped in with three or four others; they pretty much destroyed the place. There wasn't much left after that."

"Four people attacked and destroyed the school you were attending?"

"Yes, well, as it turned out, we didn't really put up much of a fight. Mostly we stood in a circle around this secret agent guy and he would flip us, or whack us on the head as each of us took our turns attacking him. He was real good."

"Okay, I guess I get the picture there ... sort of, but this next item ... you worked on a boat of some sort?"

"Yes, let me see, that was Scaramanga's stealth ship. He had these nuclear cruise missiles he'd stolen from the Russians. That was the rumor anyway. I had a great job adjusting dials on this huge metal control panel. We even wore white lab coats. It was perfect. Didn't last long though."

"I see that one was only for about six weeks. What happened there?"

"I'm not really sure what caused it, but we were going along fine, adjusting dials, looking at all the lighted panels and stuff, and all of a sudden, wham, the whole ship is rocking and bucking under us."

"That must have been terrifying."

"Yes, it was. The control panel started sending out these huge geysers of sparks and then it caught on fire and exploded. I was thrown into the sea and picked up later by a British destroyer."

"You are lucky to be alive Mr. Ozawa. That sounds like quite an experience!"

"All in a day's work."

"Hmm. Now this last job, third henchman for Dr. Glowfinger? What happened there? It was easily your best paying job."

"It was the best position I've had to date. My job was to stand next to this rotating metal chair that Dr. Glowfinger would sit in with his cat. Both Ernie Belofsky and I were guards for him whenever he sat in the chair. Ernie's the one who recommended you."

"Ernie, yes, of course, a very nice man. I met with him yesterday. Well anyway, what prompted you leave that job?"

"On that one, the giant laser weapon Dr. Glowfinger was building blew up somehow. I'm not sure why, but we barely escaped the underground cave. Hot magma and all that sort of thing, very nasty."

"I see. I think I'm beginning to understand. Well you know of course, Daniel, that we always check references for our candidates. In fact earlier today we called Dr. Glowfinger's personal assistant and he spoke glowingly of you. Your qualifications may not be conventional but they are unique."

"Thank you."

"Well then, if you are ready to retain us ..."

"Certainly. Yes."

"I do have a couple of opportunities. Let's see here ... yes, a gun-toting thug job, with a small megalomaniac who's putting together a globe-threatening nuclear device. And a really exciting long-term posting on a space station containing a high density microwave transmitter."

"They both sound interesting. Of course after my history, Jenny – that's my wife – would be quite comfortable with either the gun-toting or the microwave radiation. And she and I both like that kind of cozy, small-team feel. The question really is one of benefits. You see, we're planning a family ..."

SCHOOL NIGHT

Weed leaned over the cafeteria table towards Michael and whispered, "Here she comes, man."

Together the two 15-year-olds turned and watched 17-year-old Peggy Anderson walk provocatively towards the seniors' end of the room. Their heads moved like two people watching a tennis match in slow motion, mouths agape, staring at her tan legs and tight T-shirt as she moved across towards the popular kids' table.

"Fuck man, that is one awesome mama," Michael said softly.

"No shit man, she's the most amazing babe in the whole school," Weed agreed, never taking his eyes from Peggy who now seated herself (with an appropriate flounce of her blond hair) next to Mr-All-America, captain of everything, honors student, so-perfect-you-could-just-puke Craig Phillips.

"Well one thing's for sure, us freshman dweebs will never, and I repeat never, have a chance at a fox-unit like that," Weed concluded, turning back to his friend.

"Hey man, when we're seniors, we'll have chicks like her crawlin' all over us." Michael said with a wave of his hand.

For a moment Weed, who's real name was Widana, observed his friend wondering if the frail youngster before him could ever grow into a "senior." Michael stood only 5' 3" and weighed all of 97 pounds. His hair, a writhing chaos of dish-water blond, surrounded his pointed face which was dominated by a long, thin nose that Weed liked to call his proboscis. Perched there, just short of the end was an enormous pair of black rimmed glasses, thick as bottle caps and requiring constant push-backs, they made his eyes look 12 times their normal size. Completing the effect was a T-shirt with a picture of Garfield wearing sunglasses that said "Party Animal." Which was exactly, Weed thought, what Michael was not.

"Yah sure, the Geek and the Gook, you and me Mike, we're gonna have to fight 'em off. I believe it." Weed shook his head incredulously.

"Hey a few pounds, some push-ups ..."

"Mike, look at me, I'm Indonesian for Christ's sake, no major babe at this school is gonna want to be seen with a Gook, or even a semi-Gook."

Michael frowned, looking across at Widana. In a way, he felt the truth in his friend's words. Certainly the fact the Weed was different made a difference. He could see it in the way other freshmen treated him. But to Michael, Weed was his best and only friend. He too was small, an inch shorter than Michael and only slightly heavier. His hair was a straight and a glossy black and his almond shaped eyes would close to tiny slits when Weed laughed or smiled which was nearly all the time. Most of all, Weed was a great guy. Always interested in whatever Mike was interested in, always ready to listen and always full of plans. In a way Michael was the follower to Widana's lead, but he never felt that way. Weed's schemes were always fun and exciting, and Michael could never get over the creative imagination his friend possessed.

They went back to their lunch momentarily, making faces as they ate the unidentifiable items on their school trays.

"I got an idea the other day on how we might get some chicks," Weed said, around a mouthful of red and green jello.

"Yah?"

"Yeah man, listen, I gotta go over to the library after school and see if they have anything on what I'm thinking of. Can you come over at oh, say 6:30 or 7?"

"Maybe." Michael thought for a moment "My Mom's not too pleased with my latest performance in geometry. I gotta tell you man, getting out on a school night is gonna be a bitch."

"This is a real capper man, you gotta come over. I mean it, it's gonna be the best. We're talkin' Peggy Andersons all over the place. Sincerely!"

"What have you got in mind?" Michael asked, putting down his fork and devoting full attention to his friend.

"Don't worry about it, just come over, okay? Listen, I gotta go. I'll see you later, right?" Weed stood and looked at Michael inquisitively. Michael made no answer. "Well?"

He thought for a moment, looking back at Widana. "Yeah okay, I'll figure something out, but if this is some stroke book ... well ... I just hope it's a Hustler!" He burst out laughing.

"Way better than that, way better." Weed flashed a toothy grin and left.

Six and a half hours later, Michael found himself unable to discern what Weed might have had in mind. Weed loved to do things like this and mostly his ideas were crap, Michael thought, but every once and a while ... of course either way, they always had fun. He walked along the willow-lined Glen Summer Avenue in Pasadena only two blocks from Weed's house, enjoying the late June sun and breathing remarkably clean air. He felt somehow that this was something big though, something really spectacular. Chicks! But his anticipation ebbed as his glasses fell to the end of his nose and he pushed them back for the 100th time that day. The Geek and the Gook, that was them.

Arriving at Weed's house he knocked, then entered without waiting for Weed's mother to answer the door. She looked up momentarily, tilting her head forward to smile over granny glasses, then returned to her knitting after pointing with one of the needles toward Weed's room.

Michael rapped once on the door and flung it open yelling "Ah ha! Caught ya yankin' it, butthole," he laughed.

"You wish, butthole," Weed countered, not looking up from the book he was bent over at his cluttered desk.

Weed's room was a jumble of "early kid" and Balinese idols. The walls were adorned with grotesque masks that displayed flaring white fangs and red tongues, next to Orel Hershiser posters and an Ohio State pennant. Michael crossed the room, being sure to step on the clothes that lay scattered around the floor, and sat on the lower bunk of Weed's bed. Weed had no brother, nor did he share his room, but he preferred bunk beds and always slept on the top.

"So, where are all the babes?" Michael asked, looking mockingly under the bed and around the room. Weed only smiled.

"Just a sec."

"Is this another stupid bullshit deal of yours or ..."

Suddenly Weed stood up and turned. "I got it."

"What have you got? AIDS?"

"Fuck you bottle nose, listen this is way cool."

"Okay, I'm listening," Michael leaned forward, his chin perched on his fist.

"I found this book the other day when I was working on my English assignment. I was researching Bali, you know, my native land and all that, even though I was only two when we moved over here. Anyway, I found this book on Hindu religion in Bali."

"You called me over to talk about a bunch of cow leading, turban wearing ..."

"Will you just shut up for a second and listen?"

"Okay, get on with it," Michael sighed, rolling his eyes.

"So anyway, there are two mythical creatures in the religious dances, one is the Rangda, Rangda is sort of a ..." – Weed frowned in thought for a moment – "... a witch, I guess, is the best way to put it. In fact they call her the Witch Widow, but a really evil witch, man. For instance she likes to have men stab themselves with knives and stuff, really nasty." Weed added a grimace to his description.

"So this is the type of chicks we're gonna get? Witch ones?"

"No no, listen butthead, you wanna hear this or not?"

"Yeah okay, go on."

"The other is the Barong. The Barong is the antithesis of Rangda. He's a sort of half lion, half demon-looking dude with a long shaggy body and lots of legs. Well this Barong guy is the one for us. He does stuff like make people get along with one another and bring peace to the world. Anyway, it says here that if a man wanted to get a certain woman, he would summon the Barong on his behalf."

"Okay, I got it," Michael exclaimed. "We call up this Sarong fellah and have him call Peggy, then when it's cool, we go over and ball the snot out of her, right?"

Weed frowned. "That's not what I was talking about at all. We would summon the spirit of the Barong and direct it toward her. According to the book, if we were near by when the Barong came close to her, the effect could be quite dazzling, ... *then* we ball the snot out of her!" Weed laughed.

"Sounds pretty easy to me, *hey Barong old buddy, let's take a walk over to Peg's, what ya say*?" Michael called out to the ceiling.

"It's not quite that easy, Mike. The problem is that when you summon the Barong, Rangda has a habit of showing up, you know, to defeat the forces of good and all that. Now if Rangda shows up ..."

"Then we bang the shit out of the ugly bitch, then head over to Peggy's, right?"

"Wrong, Rangda eats our faces off, then melts our brains and we never get a date again," Weed concluded somberly.

"Okay now seriously, just what are you planning here?"

"Well, according to this we can summon the Barong with a certain group of chants and prayers, which I found in this other book." Weed briefly lifted a faded red book entitled "Balinese Dances and Rituals" by D.M. Padura.

"Once he's here, we just guide him towards Peggy's and voila, instant serious female!"

"And this will, of course, work flawlessly," Michael chided.

"Yes," Widana said simply.

They stared at each other for a moment then Michael stood and crossed the room to where Weed sat at his desk.

"Okay Weed, why not. Let's do some chanting."

It took nearly an hour to set Weed's room up to his satisfaction for the ceremony. He pulled the masks off the wall, deeming one Rangda and one Barong, laid them at either end of the bed, set up incense sticks at various spots in the room and hung colored cloth over the lights. None of this was called for in the ceremony, except the masks, but both Michael and Weed wanted the atmosphere to be right. The plan was to summon the mythical creature then lead it one block south and one block west to 124

Black Oak, home of said Peggy Anderson. There, they would decide how to get near her, but for now it was enough to just set up the room.

"Okay, now you sit on the bunk and I'll sit here on the floor," Weed said seriously, "When I give the signal we start the chant, but first, we have to clear our minds of any negative thoughts. If we have even the least amount of fear or chaos in our minds we risk the wrath of Rangda and you know what that means."

"Yeah, no faces ... I got it. Happy thoughts, okay fine." Michael said, but deep inside he wondered. What if this was for real? Weed was a strange guy some times, but this could be something pretty scary, and even if the Barong was to show up, who wanted some lion, reptile, snaky-looking thing following you down the street? Michael's anxiety increased as he thought of the pictures Weed had showed him of Rangda and the Barong, and he looked now at the masks lying on the bed in the eerie light. They seemed to take on frightening shapes.

Weed signaled that they were to close their eyes and think calming thoughts, although Michael became more agitated by the minute. But as Weed began to chant the mantras that would summon the Barong, he felt strangely calmed and his heart slowed to a dull, rhythmic thump.

For several minutes nothing happened. Then, as if a window had been opened on an autumn day, a cold wind flooded the room, lifting the blankets hanging down before Michael's head. He looked up momentarily, disbelieving what he saw, then returned to the chanting.

The air grew steadily colder.

Fear swelled inside Michael's head like a blossoming flower and he realized he'd closed his eyes. He forced them open against an almost overwhelming force. Once they were partially opened, he saw it and his eyes went wide. Leaning over the bent form of Weed was a tall hideous creature, with billowing smoke rising from the tangled crimson hair on its head. Michael could scarcely breathe, watching in terror as the creature reached down with a dripping clawed hand toward his friend's head.

"Uh, uh, uh ... Wa wa ..." He tried desperately to call out, to warn him, but he choked and gasped on the words.

The creature stopped for a moment, then began to turn slowly around, hearing Michael trying to scream.

Its face was a stark white, dominated by bulging, bloodshot eyes whose pupils looked as if they were on fire. It opened its mouth revealing blunt, curved fangs that overlapped sharp upper teeth. A bit of drool escaped its lips, hanging for a moment on the pointed chin of what could only have been the Witch Widow, Rangda.

"Oh fuck man ... this ain't real," Michael finally spit out. "You aren't real, you're a figment of our imagination!"

Rangda took a step closer and began to grin.

Weed, hearing Michael, finally looked up and saw the vision of evil before him.

"Mike, run man, run ... Shit, it's *Rangda* ... Run Mike, out the window, jump for it!" he screamed.

Mike had only a second to think as Rangda lurched forward and took a swipe at his head. He dodged to one side, scooting across the bunk and staggered toward the window behind and to the right of the bed. Weed had already crossed the room and slid the window open.

"Go Mike, *go*!" Weed shouted, fairly pushing Michael head over heels through the window and into the garden below.

Michael fell into the soft dirt, scratching himself on a rose bush, then rolled onto the lawn. A moment later Weed sprung through the window and Mike glimpsed one of Rangda's talons as it ripped open Weed's pant leg trying to catch the fleeing boy. Weed jumped up and pulled Michael to his feet and the two boys began to run. Behind them they could hear the monster clawing its way out the window, but now all they could think of was flight.

They ran south on Glen Summer, arms and legs pumping, both boys in a dead run. Michael was sure he could hear the Witch Widow now, closing on them. At any moment they would be torn to shreds by those foul claws.

They rounded the corner of a hedge onto Emerson Way and plunged through just in time to run smack into a young girl on a bicycle. All three went to the ground in a heap.

"Run girl ... It's Rangda ... Run!" Weed shouted, trying to regain his feet.

"Girl! Who're you callin' girl, geek?"

"Oh my god!" Michael exclaimed and for a moment he forgot all about the hideous beast, and all he could think about was the girl before him, indignantly brushing off her perfectly tanned legs and smoothing her clinging white shorts. They'd just run into Peggy Anderson.

They both stood, Michael's glasses half off his face and Widana's black hair standing on end, staring at Peggy and expecting Rangda any moment. But the moment never came.

"What the hell are you two twerps doing out here at this time of night? Isn't it past your bedtime or something?" she teased. "And on top of it all, you nearly run me down, then go screaming about some Ringa or Ranga or something. Jeezzzus, gimme a break, guys." She turned and began to ride away. She had barely gotten started when a huge shaggy dog burst from the bushes and crossed directly in front of her. She slammed on her brakes, nearly going head first over the handlebars. "Shit!" she exclaimed softly, then glanced back at the two boys still gaping at her, and rode away.

An hour later found them back in Weed's room, which looked completely undisturbed, other than the window, and Weed's leg showed no sign of the wicked scratch Rangda's claws would have left.

"We must'a fallen asleep and had a nightmare or something. That's the only explanation." Michael said.

"Yeah," Weed admitted, "I guess you're right. I'm still kinda scared though. You wanna spend the night?"

"Nah, sorry Weeds, can't tonight. I gotta git."

"Okay man, see you tomorrow."

"Yeah. Okay, see ya."

"Hey, be careful on the way home Mike, okay?"

Michael smiled weakly, then left.

The next day at lunch neither had much to say. They sat across from each other eating and looking around, both afraid to speak about the night before. "I just think we must have ..." Michael began.

"Listen, forget it Mike. Who knows what happened. All I know is I ain't trying that shit again ... uh uh, not ever."

"You guys mind if I sit here?" a soft voice inquired.

They turned as one and looked up to see Peggy Anderson standing at the end of their table, smiling sweetly and holding her lunch tray.

"Suuuu...uh, sure, I mean *sure*," Weed exclaimed.

Peggy sat, repeating the flounce of her perfect tresses, and looked from one to the other.

"You know, after that dog – or whatever it was – almost ran into me and I looked back at you guys, I ... well, I don't know," she said sliding closer to Weed. "I just had these ... thoughts!"

THIEVES

"Start from the beginning, Mr. Blackman," he said. But then, psychiatrists always say that, don't they?

"Well, that's the hard part," I answered truthfully. "I really don't remember when it started."

"Well in these cases there is almost always an origin for the problem. By understanding the origin, we can perhaps come to some understanding of a solution. Can you not remember anything that might be relevant?"

I thought for a moment. "It could have been some isolated incident on either of our part ... I guess it doesn't really matter where or when it started, the fact is that it did and that's all that matters."

"Alright, Mr. Blackman ... can I call you John?" I nodded my approval from my position on Dr. Liebensetzer's couch. "Good ... well then, John," he paused, "tell me at least about the first so-called *incident* that you remember."

"Okay, let me think ... I can remember one Christmas ... must have been, oh 15 years ago or so."

"Good. Go on please," he prodded.

"I had been given a neon sign by a friend of mine. A girl friend as I recall. Anyway, I was really proud of it. It was a beer sign – you know – *Coors* or something similar."

"Was this girl someone your friend Monty knew as well?"

"Hm, I don't remember. I think so. We were all in school at Northwestern together, so I suppose so, but to tell you the truth, I don't remember either way. I'm reasonably sure he wasn't interested in her if that's what you're asking."

"Not really, go ahead. You got the sign for Christmas and ..."

"It was at a party. We had lots of parties at the house I was sharing at that time. It was a big house, near the campus and ... well anyway, we had parties. You know, keg of beer, invite girls only since the guys always showed up anyway ... that sort of thing. So we had this party and Ellen – that was her name, yes, Ellen – Ellen shows up with this beer sign and gives it to me. I was ecstatic."

"Why would a beer sign ..."

"It wasn't just the sign, although I used to love that stuff. It was her as well. I'd been chasing her around for almost a month, and for her to give me a Christmas gift, well ... it was clearly an invitation."

"Invitation?" I could almost hear him peering over his glasses in that psychiatrist "What-are-you-nuts?" sort of way.

"I'm getting off the track and this is expensive."

"Go on Mr. Blackman."

"John, please call me John. For $300 per hour, you can call me John."

"Very well, John. Please continue."

"So I put this sign up in my room. Strategically above the bed, if you know what I mean. I figured I would take Ellen up there later and say, 'Hey, look at where I put your sign. Real cool huh, now take off all your clothes!'"

"This was your technique for seduction?"

"Who cares, it didn't work anyway, because when I got up there with her, it was gone."

"And ..."

"She was kinda pissed. I told her I was taking her to see the sign she gave me, and when we get there, it's gone. Of course, she figures I've already forgotten where I put it and the only reason I've invited her up there at all is to put it to her."

"Was that not the case?"

"True on both counts. I figured that in my drunken state I must have put it somewhere else. It wasn't like I was taking her up to my room to show her my interior-decorating skills, let's face it. The bottom line is that she got sort of upset by the whole thing."

"What happened next?"

"Well she left rather hurriedly, and I never did get a chance to explain it to her properly."

"And how did you find out what had happened to the sign?"

"Oh, it was about a week later. I was over at Monty's for some poker on a Friday night. There were about five of us as I recall, sitting around his kitchen table. All of the sudden Monty leaps up from his seat and announces that he has something to show us."

"This was the sign I presume?"

"Yeah. It was." I paused, trying to put that moment into words.

"I just couldn't believe my eyes. When Monty brought it out, he was showing it around to everyone, but he kept his eyes on me, as if he was just begging me to say something. I remember someone asking where he had gotten it."

"His answer?"

"Oh, I think he said a garage sale or something like that. But what I do remember was that he said it was a steal. You know, like a bargain, only he said it very specifically: 'It was a real steal,' looking right at me."

"Do you think he was taunting you?"

"No. I don't really think so; more of a game of his. Knowing him like I do now ... after 18 years I mean. I just know how he likes to play games. So I figured this was one of them."

"Games? Can you be more specific?"

"Poker, chess, checkers, any kind of games. He was always giving parties centered around games. He even had his own Las Vegas night, for God's sake."

"And what was your relationship with him at that time?"

I started to sob. The word relationship brought back so much of the pain. "Uh ... excuse me doctor. I'm sorry," I sniffed, barely containing my tears.

Dr. Liebensetzer offered me a monogrammed handkerchief. I pressed out a grim smile and blew my nose, all the time thinking I was soiling this guy's $35 handkerchief. At these rates, it was poetic justice.

"Go on please Mr. Bla ... excuse me, John."

"We were buddies then. I guess you'd call us that. We went to football games together, parties, damn near everything."

"Let's move on. When was the next incident?"

"There were some little things along the way, but it was nearly five years later when I pulled a real big one on him. I suppose it's fair to say that I'm the one who escalated things."

"What was it that you took?"

"His stereo. Not just a stereo, but a beautiful Nakamichi rig that had to have cost him five grand minimum." I found myself so wrapped up in the story I couldn't stop. "It was really something; the theft I mean. I planned it just like a real criminal mastermind. I tell you it was brilliant.

"We had been invited to a party that night. I can remember the date: June 15th, a Saturday. It was a beautiful summer evening and we were off to a barbecue. Monty and I had an apartment together at the time, near Brentwood in Los Angeles. He was taking some graduate classes at UCLA and I was going to Northridge for my MBA. Anyway, we go to this barbecue up in the Valley. I had made arrangements with some guys I knew from school to come over while we were gone and move the stuff into my room. It was perfect."

"And what was his reaction?"

"It wasn't his reaction when we got home that was priceless." I started to giggle despite my depression. "What was great was during the party, I just kept looking over at him, no matter where he was in the room, and smiling at him. It was absolutely the best. He couldn't figure out what was going on. The whole night he kept coming up to me and looking at me with his head cocked. 'You up to something?' he'd say. And I would just smile."

"And after you left the party?"

"Well, we got home about oh, 12:30 or so. And I had this girl with me – I can't remember her name – but anyway, I say 'Let's go up to my room and listen to some music,' and she says 'Okay' and off we go. Next thing I'm upstairs with *his* stereo in *my* room absolutely cranked! Blasting Eric Clapton halfway down the block.

"So he comes running up the stairs and practically leaps headlong into my room, then just stops dead. He looks at me, then at her, then at the stereo. He just stares at it for maybe 20 seconds or so, then starts to laugh."

"He laughed at you stealing his stereo?"

"That's just it. By then it was a game and I'd won that round. I'd taken the system and completely set it up as my own, all without him getting the slightest clue until I actually had it. That was the game, to steal the other guy's thing and only have him know it when you wanted him too. And by that time it was too late."

"Why was it too late? He could have easily called your bluff right then."

"But you see, that's the whole point. I had the stereo all set up as if it was mine, claimed it was mine and even took someone in to show them it was mine. If he had said something in front of the girl that would have been breaking the rules of the game. He would have embarrassed me in front of her and we were buddies. He'd never do that and I suspect, even now, with all that has passed between us ... we're still buddies." I choked on the last few words.

"This whole thing seems to centered around the material aspects of your lives. What was it that caused it to move away from that?"

I had to think about that one. What was it? What could cause such great friends as Monty and me to let things get to the state they were in? I found I had no answer. Finally, I simply shrugged from my position lying on the couch.

"Well, tell me what you think was –" the psychiatrist thought for a moment, "– the real crisis point for you."

"Ok. I guess to tell you that, I should move ahead to about one year ago." The going was tough from here, I wasn't sure what I could say about what had happened. "He got married about two years ago. To a really special girl named Wendy."

"How did *you* take this marriage?" That question threw me. I had never really thought about it in just that way.

"Well ... it was ... well, I guess it sort of signified an ending for me and a beginning for Monty. You see, by this time we had become inseparable. We were always together, we lived together, did everything together. In fact, I had transferred to UCLA and was taking classes there, although I must admit that it was kind of pointless."

"Pointless?"

"Yes. I had given up on my MBA by that time." I tried to frame the words. "I had really given up my whole direction in life. Maybe some of it had to do with him seeing Wendy; they had started dating sometime the year before, but I really think I was just sort of lost at the time. I didn't really know what I wanted to do with my life."

"What happened next?"

"Monty got a job right out of school with Lockheed. And he, Wendy and I would see each other about two or three times a week I suppose."

"Where were you living at the time?"

"I guess that's another thing that bothers me. I moved home. It was not good for the ego, let me tell you."

"Go on."

"Well, we'd see each other now and then, as I said, then one day I just found myself calling Wendy during the day. You know, when I knew Monty wasn't home. I asked her to lunch or something, I've forgotten now what it was."

"And her reaction?"

"I was mildly surprised, but she said okay and out we went. The specifics are kind of fuzzy from there, but we sort of started seeing each other, completely innocently of course, and quite often."

"How did Monty feel about this?"

"He didn't know."

"Hm. I see. Was this deliberate on your part?"

"No ... well truthfully, I would have to say yes, I suppose. At least I didn't *tell* Wendy to tell him. Neither of us ever brought it up."

"And you were attracted to her?"

"Not at first. But it became overwhelming after a while. So finally the inevitable happened. We made it on *his* bed at *his* house."

The doctor paused now and lit a meerschaum pipe.

"There were feelings of remorse?"

"Tremendous; on both our parts. In fact we vowed afterwards that it would never happen again."

"And did it?"

"Yes ... the next day."

"I see. So the infatuation did not subside after the conquest was over?"

"No, in fact I fell more and more in love with Wendy every day. And we were together nearly every day. Since I didn't have a job at the time, I could spend just about as much time with her as I wanted. So I did."

"How was this situation resolved?"

"Well that's why I'm here today. It was Thursday last. I can hardly talk about it, it's just too ..." I started to weep again.

"Please John, we're at the crux of the problem here. Let's finish it out. Please continue."

I looked up at him and sniffed, "Alright. Okay."

"Wendy and I decided that Thursday, we would tell him. You see, we'd decided to get married. She was going to leave Monty, get a quickie divorce or something; we hadn't really worked it out. We only knew we loved each other." I started to sob once more. Taking a deep breath, I continued. "I went over to their house at about seven that night. We all sat in his living room and we told him. I guess it was actually Wendy that finally spoke up. She came over and sat next to me, then just looked him in the eye and told him the whole bloody story."

"What did Monty do?"

"He stood up and started to ... well, sort of pace. He had this incredibly weird expression on his face the entire time. This lasted about a minute or so, but it seemed more like an hour. I was dying inside. Finally, he turned to us with this huge grin on his face and just started roaring with laughter."

"He laughed when you told him your were running off with his wife?"

"Yeah, it was absolutely nuts. Anyway, he looks at me and says 'So John, you think you've really pulled off the ultimate don't you? You've actually stolen my wife.' I started to stammer something about this-has-nothing-to-do-with-the-game, and he shut me up with a wave of his hand. 'Oh yes,' he said, 'This has everything to do with the game! I must hand it to you though, you did win this round, but now the game's over, John. Now it's over.' And that's when I saw her."

"Saw who?"

I barely heard him speaking to me, as if he was far away. Re-living the moment brought back such utter pain. I could scarcely go on.

"John? Go ahead, John, finish it."

I looked up at Dr. Liebensetzer through a haze of tears.

"I saw her, standing behind him, looking around the corner of the doorway to the bedroom. She was wearing a housecoat. One I recognized. Then she moved up next to him and put her arm around him, and let her eyes meet mine. I could only spit out ... 'Mom?' and she just started to slowly nod her head."

THE LETTER

Henry Thomas was walking home alongside his two good friends, Max Weiland and Terry Matthews. All three 10-year-olds were covered with mud, and Max, a few inches taller than the others, held a battered Miami Dolphins football beneath his arm. His stick-thin arms swung in time with his hitching gait. Heavy rains over the last few days had made for an ideal football field, where footing was non-existent and all players became roughly equal. Henry, walking on Max's left, was thin and had brown hair to match his deep brown eyes. His once-white shirt was torn and smeared with reddish mud and his Levi jeans were soaked through. Terry, on Max's other side, carried at least 20 pounds more than either of the others and wore a shock of red hair that seemed to have a life of its own. His face had a huge slash of red where he'd planted it during a mad dash to the end zone, and mud caked his forehead. Terry was grinning from ear to ear as he nearly always did.

The boys had played mud-football with some other friends for several hours, only giving up near three o'clock in the afternoon when Billy Watkins had broken down into tears after falling face first into the muck for at least the 100th time. The three were laughing and walking the eight or so blocks from the park back to Terry's house, where they expected to find no adults home and plenty of that nectar of the gods; Coca Cola. It was Christmas Eve.

"What's Santa bringing you this year, Max? Coal?" Terry laughed, his blue eyes sparkling from within the folds of his mud-spattered face.

"New bike, I think," Max answered ignoring his friend's

suggestion. "That red one at Ron's Cycles, I'm pretty sure."

"I'm gettin' a skateboard man," Henry chimed in. "I picked it out with my Mom the other day after school. She said I had to wait until Christmas so Santa could bring it, but she bought it right then and we took it back to my Dad's house in the trunk." He looked momentarily downcast. "I'm having Christmas at my Dad's this year, so I guess I won't see you guys."

"Santa could bring it – what a joke," Terry chided. "Jeez it's bad enough they make you wait, but they give you that Santa bull to swallow along with it."

"Hey man, I don't mind waiting."

"Sure, dude," Terry said, then stopped himself, not wanting to take it any further.

"What're you getting Terry? Do you know yet?" Max asked.

"Nah. Prob'ly some clothes, a couple of games, that sort of thing." Terry looked up at Henry and saw sadness in his friend's eyes. "Hey Henry, think of it this way, now you get two Christmases! And we'll see you the next day man. Don't sweat it."

Henry arrived home a little after 3:30 in the afternoon and found his little sister Anna sitting in the living room of their small home, building a tower of blocks with their afternoon baby-sitter Sylvia. Anna, the complete opposite of her brother, had white-blonde curls and pale blue eyes. Her sweet looks, however, belied the disposition of a linebacker. Anna wore her emotions on her sleeve at all times, seeming to alternately laugh and cry throughout the day with no middle ground.

"Hi Sylvia; hi puke-face, where's Mom?" Henry declared.

"I am not puke-face, puke-brain!" Anna cried, scowling at her brother.

Sylvia looked up at Henry, unaffected by the sibling greetings to which she'd long ago become accustomed, "I think she's over at your Dad's or something, but I'm not really sure. She should be back soon though ... said she'd be home around now." Sylvia glanced at her watch, "Any minute kiddo ... any minute now." A seasoned baby-sitter at 16 years of age, Sylvia was clearly ready to go home and enjoy her own Christmas.

Henry nodded but didn't answer. Turning, he walked into his room, closed the door and started stripping off his mud-soaked clothes, absently tossing them in a pile near his hamper. As he did so tears began to well in his eyes as his thoughts turned to Christmases past. Christmases when his Dad would have been home to throw the football or shoot some baskets. Christmases as a family. But nowadays Henry prided himself on his stoic acceptance of his father's absence. In his mind, if he behaved and was, well, just a good kid, it might bring his Dad back.

Putting on a pair of sweat pants and a T-shirt, Henry sat down heavily at his desk. Before him was a stack of baseball cards he'd been sorting the night before and some homework long since turned in, graded and brought home. In the center of the desk was a cigar box his father had given him. Once it held treasured fine Cuban cigars but now it was home for a treasure of a different kind. The smell of the reddish wood reminded him of happier times and thus was the perfect place to hide his little secret ... a letter. The envelope had no formal address, no return address and on its face it read simply "To: Santa Claus." Henry had long since decided no more address was necessary since no one but he would ever see this letter. Officially, Henry did not believe in Santa Claus. Being popular – or at least acceptable – made it completely impossible to believe in anything in the Santa/Easter Bunny/Tooth Fairy class. But somewhere buried deep within his heart, Henry could not let go of the feeling that magic still lived, and that by the power of hope and love alone things could be realized. That he harbored any belief at all was the real secret, not the letter itself. A secret he simultaneously spurned and cherished. It was a secret that could be shared with no one. Before opening the box he looked back at his door, making sure it was closed. If pukeface Anna came in and found him reading it again she'd go off in a tizzy and he'd suffer no end of her taunts. Any chance to ridicule her older brother was like candy to her.

Henry carefully opened the envelope, removed and unfolded the letter. The text was short, only a few words, but he read it again and again, hoping.. After a few moments he wiped his reddened eyes, refolded the paper then slid it gently back inside its envelope. Replacing the letter in the box, he took a deep breath and simply sat there, staring out of his window and trying not to think at all.

Later that evening he sat watching television with his sister and mother, his stomach dancing with anxiety and trying desperately not to ask when his father would arrive. Seemingly of its own volition, his mouth opened and out came "Mom, when's Dad coming?"

His mother looked exasperated, "I don't know, Henry, any more than the last time you asked –" she looked down at her watch "– exactly one minute ago. But it should be soon now, I think. He said around 7:00, and it's that now."

"Mommy, I don't want Henry to leave, make him stay," Anna whined from her perch on her mother's lap, her face smeared with chocolate from some tasty she had been allowed.

"I'm not staying, Anna," Henry retorted. "I'm going to Dad's for Christmas. Tell her I'm not staying Mom."

"Don't worry Anna, we'll have a nice night together," her mother said, smoothing her daughter's unruly locks.

The young girl's eyes were puffy and underscored with dark circles. She'd had no nap today. Fatigue along with a near overdose of sugar was coming to the surface of a very tired four-year-old. She began softly to whimper and cry.

"I want Henry to stayyyyyyy," her wail burst from her like water from a ruptured dam.

"I know, honey, I know," her mother held her tight and rocked her.

At that moment the doorbell rang. Anna instantly stopped crying and looked up with newly bright, clear eyes. With a quick glance at his mother, Henry leapt to his feet and ran to the door. Opening it, he looked up into the smiling face of his father.

"Daddy!" he cried, then dove forward as his father stooped to hug him.

"Hi gang ... can I come in?" his father asked, looking over Henry's shoulder.

"Yes, Clint, you can come in." His mother managed a brief smile, then stood and led Anna to her father.

"Hi sweet cakes," he said to Anna. Releasing Henry, he knelt to kiss his daughter on the cheek, then picked her up as he stood.

"And what are we all up to?" he asked, trying too hard in a strained moment to keep things light.

"Just watching Rudolph the Red-Nosed Reindeer on TV for the gazillionth time," Henry's mother answered, taking a reluctant Anna back from him as he stepped into the living room.

"I'm all set Dad, let's go, okay?"

"Hold on a second, Henry," his father answered, looking away from his son. Remembering past disappointments, Henry felt an all too familiar lump begin to rise in his throat.

"Dad, come on, let's go. You said we were going to your place for dinner," Henry's voice climbed an octave and he pulled at his father's arm.

"I said hold on a second, Henry, we have some gifts to exchange and there's been a slight change in plan."

Henry's fought hard, but his eyes flooded and he choked on the massive knot now fully formed in his throat.

"Daddy? Don't we have to go?" Henry asked, barely containing his emotions, fighting to stay calm.

"Henry, you're just going to have to give it a chance here son, now please ..." Henry could contain it no further. Salty tears ran in streams down his cheeks into the corners of his mouth. His face contorted into a silent scream and he turned and bolted for his room.

"Henry, wait," his father said, making a grab for Henry's arm. He was too late and the young boy ran down the hallway and slammed the door. Even Anna dared not speak at that moment as two dumbstruck parents and one bewildered child stared after Henry in silence.

Confused and feeling utterly alone, Henry stood gasping for air, trembling and sobbing in the center of his room, too hysterical to cry out or even move. In his haste he'd not turned on the light, and the only illumination came from a small nightlight tucked neatly behind one of his dressers, where none of his friends might find it. Breathing in great heaving gulps, his tear-filled eyes rolled about the room. From the corner of his eye he spotted the cigar box and turned toward it. His face twisting into a snarl, he took the box in both hands and raised it over his head, intending to smash it against the desk and so forever ridding himself of the treachery of silent hope buried inside. The top fell open and Henry looked up expecting to see the letter fall free. But nothing came out. The letter was gone.

More than ever in his life, Henry was spinning out of control. His mind reeled, unable to grasp what his eyes were seeing. How could his letter, his most private secret, be gone? He'd looked at it no more than an hour ago and no one had been in his room since then, unless ... Then in cold fury, he realized who must have taken it.

"Annnnnaaaaa!!!" he shrieked, striding to the door, throwing it open and racing back down the hallway shouting "Anna!" and then, rounding the corner into the living room, "You took my letter!"

What he saw dazed him further. Through the mist of tears and rage he looked at the three members of his family standing in the living room staring back at him. They were standing together. His father's arm was around his mother's shoulders and Anna was in between.

"Wha ... what's going on?" Henry asked, dumbfounded, not registering the stack of suitcases standing in the doorway.

"What's going on, Henry," his father announced calmly, his own eyes filling with tears, "is that I'm home, son. Home for Christmas, home for ..." Unable to find words, Clint Thomas stepped forward and swept his limp and weeping son into his arms. He smiled into Henry's eyes, kissed him gently and said, "I'm home."

Henry has a family of his own now, and not a Christmas goes by that he doesn't walk quietly out to the mailbox and deposit one of his own children's wish-lists into the care of the U.S. Postal Service. And whenever he does, from somewhere in the deepest reaches of his mind comes a memory – part dream and part waking – of a tender, gloved hand stroking his forehead that fateful night as he drifted into blissful sleep and saying softly, "To all a good night."

PART 2

MERLIN

The smile on Dr. Ralph Kiner's face had been plastered there for more than three days and he had good reason to smile. He sat, leaning back in his office chair, surrounded by four walls, bare except for one snapshot of his cat Merlin. The more he thought about getting serious, the more he grinned, occasionally chuckling out loud. The room was small, but that never bothered Ralph and it was only one of 106 on that floor of NASA headquarters in Houston, which also failed to cause him any remorse. The reason for his mood wasn't the fact that no one had bothered him since his translation system had been completed; or the satisfaction that comes with a job well done. It wasn't the final victory over Smithson in the design of the system that would allow mankind to communicate with the first alien to land on Earth, no; it was something much more mundane. He'd been allowed to bring Merlin to work. And that made him smile.

Merlin on the other hand could not have appeared more bored. Mostly black, Merlin had two white front paws and enormous green eyes which were closed at the moment. He was sleeping atop Ralph's printer basking in the warmth it generated and if anyone could have asked him, Merlin would have said that things were just fine with the world.

Ralph leaned forward with a sigh and absently reached up to scratch Merlin. The cat accepted by lifting his head, eyes still closed and pushing into Ralph's fingers. In just fifteen minutes it would be time to leave for the conference room where a being from the depths of interstellar space awaited its chance to hobnob with the dwellers of Earth. But Ralph was in no hurry. His job was complete, having made the final adjustments in the system interface the previous day. His presence would be needed only to type in commands, and in case of a malfunction in the translator he'd built – something he was quite sure was impossible.

Suddenly the door to his office burst open, startling Merlin and breaking an otherwise serene silence. Ralph was confronted with the sweating face of Iver Smithson, his sometime colleague and more often rival. Smithson, a rotund man of middle age, was the complete opposite of Ralph Kiner. Where Kiner was tall and had an unruly mass of brown hair, Smithson had almost no hair and seemed to grow in girth nearly every day. Ralph's clothes hung on him like a clinging moss while Iver's garments seemed ever at the bursting point. It was all he could do to squeeze in the door and past Ralph's desk. Smithson, panting heavily, dropped himself in the lone folding chair across from Ralph and fixed him with beady blue eyes. "What the hell are you doing sitting here like a veg', Ralph? The conference is in 10 minutes for Christ's sake!"

"Calm down, Iver, we have at least fifteen minutes and besides, you're just going to be a spectator anyway. So relax, man, enjoy the limelight while we have it."

"Jeez Ralph, how can you stay so damn calm about all this? I mean, we got an honest-to-God alien upstairs! Doesn't that get you the least bit excited?"

"I'm ecstatic but I don't need to go rushing around like a crazed madman. Look Iver, we've done our part, now let's sit back and enjoy, okay?"

Merlin, who had sought shelter under the desk, re-emerged now and jumped up on Ralph's lap en route to his station on top of the printer. The mere sight of the cat made Smithson's eyes water and his sinuses began to swell.

"Aw shit Ralph, I thought they made you leave that hair bag at home, what's he doing here?" Iver said, squinting against a flood of streaming tears.

"Merlin has official permission to occupy this office with me," Ralph declaimed, holding a barely tolerant Merlin against his chest, "and you, Iver, do not. So please leave so I can prepare myself ... and here's a handkerchief," he said holding one across the desk. "Pull yourself together man, we're about to meet a real live alien!"

Smithson heaved himself erect, barely managing an indignant sigh among the clogged nasal passages and pushed himself out the door. Quiet once more descended on Ralph's office and Merlin resettled himself on the warm printer. Ralph shook his head slowly, then put his hands behind his head, leaned back and let his smile return. Yes, everything was just fine.

It was nearly 40 minutes later when the conference actually got under way. Ralph arrived late as usual, and as usual the conference was held up for the arrivals of various senators, chair-persons of this and administrators of that. The room was a great oval, now dominated by a large smoky grey cylinder against the far wall. The conference table formed a giant horse-shoe with its ends nearly touching the alien's eco-chamber. Around it were faces of men and women bobbing to and fro above nameplates announcing their title and right to attend. Ralph could only continue to smile as he leaned, arms folded against one of the rear walls opposite the cylinder. The inventor of the translator was not one of the chosen nameplate dignitaries.

The NASA director was a diminutive man with dark features and Ben Franklin glasses that he was sure made him look intelligent. He stepped up to a podium at the apex of the horse-shoe table and peered over his glasses at the buzzing room.

"Gentlemen, ahem ... and ladies, please ... may I have your attention?" The director spoke into a microphone, his amplified voice barely noticeable above the din. The noise level dropped only slightly as people glanced his way then returned to their excited conversations.

"We are about to begin – may I have your attention please!" The director spoke again, more adamantly. The noise dropped after a moment then a developed into pregnant silence that engulfed the room. All eyes were upon the cylinder now, as the director began.

"Today is easily the most momentous event in the history of mankind." He stopped and looked around the room for emphasis. "Today, ladies and gentlemen, we in this room will actually communicate with a being from another planet. Doctors Kiner and Smithson, are you with us? Please take a bow for your incredible work in creating the translation system."

Ralph only continued to smile. Smithson, in another corner of the room, also without a nameplate, waved madly, grinning so hard Ralph was sure his face would burst.

"Thank you gentlemen, all of Earth thanks you. Now – on to our guest of honor. Before me you see a cylinder which holds a small pocket of our guest's own atmosphere. Rather toxic stuff I'm told, mostly ammonia and free sulfurous compounds. Attached to the side, where you see the lights, is the interface designed by our people. It runs to our main Neural Net where the alien's communications can be translated into human speech. We will hear his "words" (though I am told it's more like a radio transmission we listen to) through the loudspeaker system in here. We can then communicate our responses to it via the same computer interface." The director consulted his notes for a moment then resumed, "I guess there's not much more to say so if you will, Dr. Kiner, let us begin."

Ralph walked calmly over to the keyboard and terminal where he would enter the queries and responses to the alien. He entered a code, and the system responded by opening a dialog window. Over the loudspeaker came the alien's odd synthesized voice.

"I am ready," it said simply.

"Dr. Kiner, we would like to ask it where its home system is, can you do that for us?" the director asked, leaning into his microphone.

Ralph did not respond, but typed in his query:

what is location of your home?

"It is ... about 1327.244 times the distance traveled by a photon in one of your years. If you can input a map of the galaxy I may be able to identify it. But I am a diplomat, not an astronomer."

Ralph looked back over his shoulder at the director and raised his eyebrows.

"Ask it whether ..." the director's question was interrupted by the alien.

"I wish to speak to a member of the ruling class of beings on this world. Please arrange this."

The room made a collective gasp. "Quiet please, quiet!" the director ordered. "Dr. Kiner, please inform the alien that we are the ruling class," the director sputtered. "What could he possibly ..."

we are the ruling class. please continue.

Ralph typed in.

"Inaccurate. We are aware of at least five higher species. Please do not toy with us. We have come a long way."

Ralph began to sweat. What the alien had said was certainly a less-than-veiled threat. If we could not convince the alien of our superiority, what could they do? Their massive ship, now in orbit around the Earth might hold untold weapons capable of who knows what, planetary sterilization! What could we do against that? He knew the group in this room, filled with diplomats and stuffed shirts would be incapable of handling the situation. Ralph decided to act on his own. Without looking back at the director he began to type ...

where do you get the knowledge of our ruling class?

"Your communications. Primarily something called television."

Ralph turned to the buzzing room and as he did so, utter silence was restored. All eyes fell upon him. In his quiet, unamplified voice he said, "They watch TV."

"TV!" the director shouted. "Well tell them that's not real ... I mean tell them ..." The room erupted in a cacophony of shouting and hysteria. No one even noticed when the door to the conference room opened slightly to permit the entry of Merlin the cat, who spotted his master instantly and the warm computer he was sitting at.

Ralph turned back to his terminal trying desperately to think of a way to convince the alien of the truth.

can you tell us what the other species are?

was all he could think to type in.

"Dolphins, Whales..."

those are aquatic species

Ralph typed as Merlin walked past, momentarily rubbing himself against Ralph's legs. The cat stopped just past the desk where the terminal sat and tensed himself to jump. Ralph allowed himself a wry smile at Merlin's approach, but hastily continued typing.

can you cite land dwellers?

At that moment Merlin made his leap and landed on a jumble of wires near the rear of the machine, tearing several loose from their connections. Ralph's screen went blank.

"Merlin! For God's sake, what are you up to ..." Ralph's voice trailed off as the alien's voice came over the speaker.

"Thank you, we may now proceed," it boomed.

"Ralph! What the hell's that cat doing ..." The director suddenly saw the same thing that had transfixed the audience a second earlier. Merlin stood now, atop the terminal, his huge green eyes slowly taking in the room. Into each person's mind the same astonishing thought made its indelible way, loud and clear ...

"I'll take over from here," Merlin said.

GOT A LIGHT?

There were three things Callamoor needed to know that he did not. The first was that his ship was about to have some trouble with its stardrive. A second had to do with his general lack of knowledge regarding stardrive repair. And most important, was that the planet Earth has no repair facilities for Mark 7 nebula hoppers. Had he known any one of these three, he probably would not have tried to take a shortcut through the spiral arm of a rather unremarkable galaxy called the Milky Way.

"So, it's been, oh ..." Carl looked down at his watch, "twelve minutes, Arnie. Going for a personal record?" Arnie, shaking now in the fight to deny his craving for a cigarette, leaned over his Salisbury steak and pointed a skeletal finger at Carl.

"I gone a far sight longer than twelve, Carl. Now just shut your face whilst I chew my way through this poor excuse for a piece of meat."

Florida Jones, who owned Steve's Big Time Diner, scowled at Arnie. "Now whatcha doin' complainin' 'bout my Salisbury steak? You order it every damn night and you know I ain't changed the damn recipe in 15 damn ye-ahs?" She paused, shaking her head then crossing her meaty dark brown arms across the dirty pink of her apron. Florida stood just 5'3" tall, including her gray streaked pile of wire-brush hair, but she took no sass from anyone, especially Arnie. No doubt her 180-plus pounds of solid, working-woman flesh was more than a match for Arnie's "Barney Fife" physique. "Somethin's wrong with you boy. Somethin's definitely wrong with you."

Arnie glanced up at her then shot a furtive look at the battered screen door that led to freedom and a chance to smoke. Eyes dropping once again to his plate, he felt the iron grip of addiction begin to course through his body. Returning to his food, he tried unsuccessfully to cover his shaking hands by forcefully sawing through the meat on his plate.

The inside of the Diner hadn't changed much in the twenty-some years that Carl, Medium Melvin and Arnie had been coming in; and Arnie knew the sound that door would make when it slammed behind him. More importantly, he knew the barking laugh and taunts he would shortly have to endure about his smoking habit, once the nicotine became irresistible. He leaned forward over his plate and glanced at Carl, finishing his third Hamm's. Carl grinned back, his beet-red swollen face folding around yellow teeth, beneath a bulbous nose. Medium Melvin sat in the middle of the two; an arrangement they had silently worked out over the years to insure Arnie's health when Carl's temper went off. Melvin was only slightly smaller than Carl's 240 pounds and an inch shorter, but he could somehow calm the larger man in even the worst moments; "Medium Melvin" the moderator.

After stuffing a few more bites into his tiny mouth, Arnie could take it no more. He let out an exaggerated yawn and announced, "Think I'll just go catch a breath fellas, back in a flash." Carl grinned, wiping a bit of froth from his lip and belched loudly.

"Catch a breath, catch a breath ... what you mean is, smoke a grit – why can't you just say smoke a grit, Arnie?" Arnie tried to squeeze by the larger man and dart for the door, but Carl was too quick for him, catching Arnie's arm as he went by. "Catch a breath here, Arnie," Carl said, pulling the smaller man's face up to his then expelling another enormous burp.

"Jesus Carl, you are some kinda pig, you know that!" Arnie yelped, wiping the spittle from his face and pulling away.

Carl started to get up after him but felt Mel's hand on his arm. "Let 'im go Carl, for Christ's sake, it don't hurt you what he's doin'. Let 'im smoke it if he wants." Carl, half turned on his stool, looked back over his shoulder at Mel, then relaxed. He stared at Mel for a moment longer, sighed, then finally returned to his French dip sandwich, stuffing nearly half into his mouth in one bite.

Arnie had just cleared the door, expecting to hear the familiar slam of the aluminum screen against wood when another sound nearly knocked him flat. What appeared to be a jet fighter came roaring over the

Diner at no more than one hundred feet, blotting out the setting sun. Shielding his eyes, Arnie watched as the gray metal craft cleared the roof heading east and losing altitude. He was nearly bowled over as Carl, Melvin and Florida – in that order – came barreling out the door to see what had happened.

The dirt parking lot swirled with dust devils from the object's passing as the four ran around to the back of the Diner. They arrived, eyes watering from the grit, just in time to see the craft settle into the trees 300 yards further east.

Callamoor cursed the salesman that had sold him the Mark 7 as he watched the instruments show his ship's drop to sub-light speed. Exasperated, he extended a pseudopod to press a stud that brought up an image of the local area. The map showed only one possible landing site, and that with only a primitive culture. The atmosphere was not extremely noxious to him, though there was a rather high oxygen content, so he held some hope of getting help. At least if he could communicate with these primitives they might be able to supply him with enough information to find the galactic call box the map said was installed on this backwater planet. His only worry was about how they would react to a creature made up of a red jelly-like substance remotely akin to napalm. He had little choice in the matter however; so down he went to a hopefully soft landing.

Piling into Carl's bright red, brand new Ford pickup, Melvin, Carl and Arnie raced off down Evergreen Road toward where the jet fighter, or whatever it was, had landed. They could see the dust rising from a small clearing just off the road as they pulled even. "I think it's one of them stealth bombers they been talkin' about. Maybe they can land vertical, you know?" Arnie said as they leapt from the truck and headed into the woods.

"Bullshit, man. That's a genuine Ko-ree-un spacecraft, right here in our woods. We'll be heroes for findin' it," Carl panted as they raced toward the craft, now partially visible through the trees.

All three halted at the same time as they made the clearing. Before them sat something that looked like a cross between a George Lucas movie and a dragonfly. The body of the thing was roughly ovoid, with two large metal wing-like structures attaching to its middle. It was about 25' tall and, including its wings, about 40' wide. Its heat-scarred metal pinging and hissing, it squatted on three shining chrome-like legs suspended over the grass of the clearing. As the friends stood speechless and petrified, a ramp began slowly extending toward the ground in front of them. The only sounds now were a faint whine of gas escaping from the thing and the three men panting as they watched the ramp touch the ground, only 20 feet away.

Arnie's eyes had grown to the size of Florida's dinner plates as Callamoor extended a tentative slug-like foot down the ramp. He sucked in his breath at seeing the red blob begin its oozing progress. He shivered from head to toe. "Holy fuckin' shit!" he sputtered, turning just in time to see Carl and Melvin bolt to the truck, jump in, and race from the clearing in a cloud of dust and flying pebbles.

Callamoor advanced slowly on Arnie's quaking form. Yes, this truly was a primitive form, trapped in a permanent, immutable body. In human terms he let out a deep sigh and contemplated what he might do to communicate with this being. It was entirely possible that this would be the first time these people had ever met an alien. First contact was always rough, and Callamoor did not relish the thought of a lengthy stay.

Arnie was unable to move. His feet felt like they were trapped in deep mud as the alien approached him, doing a combination of rolling and slithering along. His body shook like an aspen tree in a windstorm and he could not even emit the scream that was building inside of him. All at once the being simply stopped. Still frozen, Arnie somehow felt a bit less threatened and now some curiosity crept into him; could this really be an alien? Inside its red jelly flesh, lights swam and ripples appeared; the being was obviously trying to communicate. But Arnie, in abject terror, could not figure how to respond. This was really it! The first human contact with an alien being – and Arnie M. Phelps was the human! Arnie's confidence rushed back to life and with it came a craving recently forgotten. A cigarette! Just the thing to calm my nerves, he thought. Pulling the pack from one pocket of his jeans and the matches from the from the other, Arnie lit his very last cigarette, and tossed the match casually to the ground.

A little too close to an unfortunate, extremely flammable alien.

PAL

The original sale of model R2400, serial number N3223-701, took place on June 2nd in the year 2064. The robot was purchased from Byron-Stamms Robotics by a loving father for his seven-year-old son who went by the name of Jaren Phillips. Jaren, immensely pleased with his new robot, named it Pal and successfully loaded the name into the machine's memory. From that day forward Pal would belong to no other family.

Nowadays obsolete, Pal was quite a revolutionary system for his day. He stood an even six feet tall and, including accessories, weighed upward of 570 lbs. Other than having a skin of shining chromium alloy, Pal was man-like in shape. Certain key features were omitted of course; fully "functional" robots were still 25 years away. He had no facial features, hair or ears, but put a funny-nose and glasses on him, along with a hat, and he could do a remarkable Groucho Marx impersonation. Pal could teach nearly any subject beneath the graduate level. He was purchased with a package that included over 75 languages and dialects, in which he could speak, read and write. Most of all, however, Pal was a protector and friend to young Jaren.

Each day, after school, Jaren would rush home, eager to tell Pal about his lessons, other children, and the happenings of the day. Pal would sit quietly, occasionally commenting or asking for illumination, a tireless listener who was truly interested in the adventures of a small boy. As the years progressed Pal became increasingly valuable to Jaren, helping with difficult lessons, encouraging him when he felt down and sometimes, simply being there. While other children became bored with their systems, Jaren's relationship with his robot grew into that singular closeness reserved only for lifetime friends and family.

One afternoon Pal and a then 13-year-old Jaren had taken a walk around his father's estate in Connecticut. They walked in silence for nearly an hour, listening, watching and absorbing the outdoors in ways only understood at Jaren's age.

"One day you will become bored with me Jaren. You mustn't forget that I am only a system," Pal stopped and turned to Jaren. "I am easily replaced."

"Aw don't be stupid Pal, I'll never get bored with you. It's like ... well ... I don't know. I guess, at least to me, you're really something special." Jaren reflected for a moment, then looked up into Pal's featureless face, "You're different than any system I've ever run into. Even the brand new ones with simulated emotions ... it's just not the same."

They began to walk again, each lost in thought and each knowing that what the robot had said was true.

At the age of 22, Jaren graduated from the academy of medical arts, and Pal watched, sitting upright and proud, next to Jaren's father, as Jaren accepted his doctoral degree. Samuel Phillips had objected when his son had asked if Pal could sit with his father, but Jaren insisted and his father, filled with pride, had acquiesced without much resistance. Pal was the only system in the audience that day and though no one in the audience noticed, his chromium hide glistened like never before.

Likewise, Pal was in the audience the day Jaren married Jennifer Seyas, seated and being served by other robots as if he were human. Pal was 23 years old that year, older than many systems but not yet obsolete. He had been upgraded six times by Byron-Stamms and worked flawlessly, but he knew he would soon have to be replaced. Robots simply did not stay with one family for this long. Pal took this realization with typical robotic indifference, waiting for the day when he would be placed with a new family or simply dismantled.

Two years later Jennifer gave birth to a son, Merrick Phillips. Merrick was a near carbon-copy of his father in appearance, but quite different in temperament.

"I just don't know what to do with him, Jaren," Jennifer Phillips began one morning at breakfast. "It seems like since he turned 11 this year he's just become a holy terror. We can't even leave him alone for a second without him tearing the place up."

"Well I'm not sure I know what to do either." Jaren let out a deep sigh, looking into his coffee cup. "Since he dismantled the cleaning unit, we sure as heck can't leave him with machines any more, and to get human help would cost a fortune."

"Well how is it that you came out so differently from your son?" she chided. " What was it that made you so sweet?"

"That's easy. I was raised by Pal." Jaren waved his hand in the direction of the robot.

"So the answer is obvious, let's give him Pal."

"No."

"Why not?" She leaned forward now across the table, searching her husband's eyes.

"Well ... what if he does to Pal what he did to the cleaning unit ... I just couldn't let that happen to him."

"To Merrick or Pal? Which one are you talking about, Jaren?"

"Pal of course. He's like a brother to me ... or even a father. I can't let Merrick tear him apart like some common cleaning device. Pal is my friend."

"Now let's get serious here, Jaren. How can Pal be your friend, or anyone else's for that matter? He's a machine, nothing more. Nuts, bolts, some solder and a metal skin." She tried again to catch his eye as he looked down at his hands on the table. "Jaren, come on now. Let's give him Pal, and tell him that the robot is his; to do with as he pleases. It may just teach him some responsibility. If nothing else, it will give Pal something to do. He's not exactly our most productive unit you know."

"I don't know Jen ..."

"It'll work out you'll see. Maybe Pal can make some headway with the boy. It certainly can't hurt."

"Well," Jaren felt a lump building in the pit of his stomach. Giving up Pal, even to his son, was something he had never even considered.

"Hey, even if the kid totally disassembles him, we can always get him put back together. Okay?"

"Okay, alright, we'll try it." Jaren finally gave in.

Pal who was nearby, as he always was for Jaren, could not keep from overhearing and understanding the conversation. He started to review memories of a much younger Jaren, preparing again to deal with the wants and needs of an 11-year-old boy.

Later that afternoon, alone in his room with Pal, Merrick sat on the bed scowling at the robot.

"So you're mine, eh? Supposed to bring me around, I suppose? Sounds like one more excuse to get that brat Merrick out of their hair to me."

"I don't see it quite that way Mer ..."

"Shut up, system. If I want you to talk I'll ask you. Until then just shut up." Merrick scowled at Pal. "You're just a 35-year-old piece of crap R2400, not worth the metal you're made of! Why I'd bet that if I called Robot Scrap they wouldn't even come and get you!" Merrick jumped to his feet and moved to confront the shining chrome shape before him. "Why couldn't they get me an A490 or one of the 500 series! I'll be the laughing stock of the entire school dragging you around."

Pal stood silently before the youngster.

"Okay robot, let's see if I can get the covers off ya. Now where are they?"

"I am not user accessible in any way except for battery recharge ... I'm sorry Merrick."

"You'll call me *master*!" the boy exploded.

"There's no reason to become agitated ..."

"I said shut up!" Merrick howled, jumping and stamping his feet. The boy's face was bright red now and he began wildly running his hands over Pal looking for an opening. "Stupid stinking robot, just wait'll I get you opened up. We'll see who gets straightened out here."

Pal stood motionless while the boy ranted, thinking of Jaren at the same age.

That night Merrick took a baseball bat to Pal, pounding the robot with one swing after another until small dents appeared covering the entire skin. He was still too short to reach Pal's head so he had to content himself with blows to the body and legs. Jaren, hearing the noise, burst into the room to find Merrick, his eyes wild and red, spittle flying from his mouth in rage as he beat Pal again and again. The robot stood motionless, absorbing each blow, making no attempt to protect himself, nor uttering the slightest sound.

"Stop it right now, Merrick! What the heck are you doing?!"

The boy continued with a barely concealed smirk at his father.

Jaren stepped forward snatching the bat away. Merrick howled and ran screaming out of the room, terrorizing the rest of the systems until Jaren could track him down. Several sleepless hours later, Merrick finally calmed enough for Jaren to put him to bed, but Jaren would sleep no more that night, replaying over and over the scene of his most faithful friend being repeatedly battered by an angry boy.

Byron-Stamms put a new skin on Pal a week later, but the old shine Pal had kept up so diligently over his years of service would never return.

At the age of 17, Merrick received a present of his first space speedster. Most other kids his age had had them for some time, but though Jaren was by now quite wealthy, Merrick's continuing bad behavior had kept him from trusting his son with anything outside the Earth's atmosphere. On that day Merrick fairly beamed.

"Dad, I just can't tell you what this means to me. It's like ... well you really trust me. I won't let you down, Dad, I swear. You did the right thing giving it to me. I'm really pleased."

"Well, I hope so son. Your mom and I have wanted to give this to you for a long time. Pal says you're finally ready for it."

At the mention of the robot, Merrick's eyes narrowed imperceptibly.

"We just wanted to be sure you wouldn't ... well ... hurt yourself ... you know what I mean." Jaren found it hard to tell his son how he felt.

Merrick dropped his eyes to the ground. "I know, Dad. I guess I've been a handful and not too responsible. But you'll see." He returned his gaze to his father. "I'll really take care of the speedster." He paused. "Listen Dad, some of the guys are going out to Io tonight. You know, to collect some ice crystals and stuff. You think I can go?"

"It's kind of a long way Mer ..."

"Oh come on, Dad, everyone's going. I can follow them out and back, it'll be okay. Come on, you gave me the speedster, let me prove I deserve it," Merrick pleaded.

"Well okay." Jaren resigned himself once again to giving in to his son. "Just be sure to take Pal with you. In case there's trouble he'll help you out."

Merrick grinned, "Yeah sure Dad, no problem. Well I gotta go, we meet in 20 minutes, see ya later." He turned on his heel and left, with Pal following dutifully behind.

Jaren stared after his son and wondered; I surely hope these reassurances are for real, I surely do.

"You there, Phillips?" The comm unit in Merrick's speedster crackled.

"Yeah, I'm here. You guys ready?"

"We're tired of waitin' for you, that's for sure. Got your R2400 baby-sitter there, asshole?"

"Shut up Leonard, let's go." Merrick spat into his comm unit as he aligned with the other boys' speedsters in Moon orbit.

They shot away towards Jupiter at terrific speeds, each jockeying for position over the others. The trip to Io, the boys' favorite meeting spot, normally took a bit over three hours to complete but tonight they made it in just under two hours 25 minutes. Their speedsters glinted in the swirling radiance of Jupiter as they set up orbits and started scanning for the best crystal hunting grounds. A fine, blue-white ammonia crystal would last many days on Earth and was a great prize among the young men. Merrick broke away from the pack quickly and swooped toward the surface of the ice-covered satellite, landing next to a deep chasm rimmed with jutting ice spires pushed up by tidal action on the moon's surface.

He popped his belt open and turned to Pal, sitting silently behind him.

"Out, robot. Get me that nice big one there off the bow," Merrick ordered.

"There are some nicer ..."

"Out, robot! When I want you to speak I'll tell you to speak. Now out!"

Pal stood slowly, his once-shining eyes dull, and turned to the airlock. Letting himself in, he cycled the air, then stepped out onto the freezing surface, impervious to the cold. Moments later he'd reached the crystals Merrick had indicated and began working the largest one back and forth, trying with his immense strength to break it free.

The thin atmosphere of Io was barely enough to carry the sound of the speedster as it lifted on gravitic motors, but Pal heard it nonetheless. The field generated by the motors forced Pal to stagger backwards and he could see Merrick was holding the speedster steady, forcing Pal further and further toward a gaping crack in the ice. Pal fought the thrust of the motors as long as he could, his self-preservation modules kicking in full force. But it was too much. Finally, he fell, his body twisting and caroming off the sheer walls of the crevasse.

Within the speedster Merrick allowed himself a smile, but only momentarily. "Pal just froze up, Dad, hadda leave him there. I couldn't very well pick him up," he'd tell his father. His grin became a mask of revenge and he turned the speedster away, heading out to rejoin his friends. Now his father would have to get him a real functional robot, not some ancient R2400.

At the bottom of the chasm, his once shining legs reduced to mere twisted metal, one arm snapped off and with a massive dent in his torso, Pal looked up at the thin ribbon of Io's sky. In his final moments, he thought of a young boy, and long walks in the Connecticut sunshine. He thought of a man he loved. Then he did something Byron-Stamms Robotics will tell you is impossible ... and died of a broken heart.

TAKE OUT

Belfin swiveled his photonic preceptors towards his beloved Zorgap. He knew she was vexed. They'd been orbiting this backwater planet called Earth for more than 50 zevs – about three Earth-days – and they still could not agree. Belfin would not give in. Zorgap knew this and was close to acquiescence, but she was holding out until the last moment, making him squirm as much as possible. And so she sat next to him, in the cockpit of their ship, her nostril slits tightly pursed and her antennae held quiescent.

Belfin reached out a long green tentacle and gently caressed Zorgap's dorsal ridge, running the tip over her lovely perception nodules. She shivered then relaxed, her skin turning the consistency of Jell-O. She had given in. Belfin reached out with all three of his large appendages and manipulated the controls of the ship sending it into a careening dive towards the surface of the planet below. His nostril slits opened wide and his antennae oscillated wildly; he was ecstatic ... and his hunger would soon be quenched.

The door to NASA operations flew open, banging against the stops on either side. It was momentarily filled by a cigar-smoking barrel of a man peering out from under dense black eyebrows with a baleful glare. William "Buck" Kirby, FBI liaison to NASA, was angry, damn angry and whoever had caused this fiasco was gonna be hung.

"Where is he?" Kirby bellowed.

A diminutive man in horn-rimmed glasses and a rumpled white shirt looked up from his computer terminal and disdainfully indicated a glass-doored office at the other end of the room.

"Damn NASA twerps," Buck muttered under his breath as he strode toward the door.

Approaching the office, he could hear a heated conversation going on within. Any arguments would soon be over, he thought, allowing a grim smile to crease his lips; he would take care of that.

As he opened the door, his smile turned to a frown and the hot air that inflated his chest shrunk to a cold lump in his throat. Before him, sitting next to NASA director Sam Phillips, was Edward Simpson, CIA, scrutinizing Kirby over Ben Franklin glasses.

"Fuck," he muttered; first the NASA twerps, then the head damn CIA twerp, and he still didn't know shit. Well, he'd soon remedy that.

"Glad you could make it William," Simpson hissed. "Take a seat and we'll fill you in."

"What I want to know is why the hell I'm just finding out about this thing. For Chrissake, this is a matter of national security ... what the fuck's ..."

"In time William," Simpson interrupted then nodded to a tall dark man, who stood next to a large screen monitor. "Continue, Dr. Majowski."

William Kirby huffed then sat down heavily and crossed two meaty arms across his chest, scowling at the CIA man.

"Well, as I was explaining to Mr. Simpson here, this thing's been orbiting the earth for about 74 and a half hours now." He indicated a blip on the monitor. "This is a simulation of course, but quite accurate and up to the minute with our tracking information. It's large, I would say roughly," he stopped for a moment, scratching the bridge of his nose. "Oh about a city block long and equally wide."

"Well what is it? North Korean? It's not those Chinese bastards is it?" Kirby bellowed, his face reddening by the second.

The CIA man glared at Kirby for a moment then nodded to Dr. Majowski.

"We're sure it's not man-made. I mean, if it is, then neither SAC, nor you folks, the NSA nor the CIA know anything about it. And I can tell you that if anyone tried to lift anything like that into orbit we'd know. No, it's not man-made." He paused for a moment, then leaned forward across the table toward the three bureaucrats.

"Gentlemen, this thing appears to be extraterrestrial in origin. In fact, we believe this may be our first contact with an alien species." He leaned back and smiled. He'd waited a long time to say those words and they tasted sweet in his mouth.

"Aw bull-shit, Dr Majohowitz ... or whatever the hell your name is, that's just pure bull. Ain't no such damn thing as aliens." Kirby's face had now passed red into crimson.

Simpson swiveled in his chair to face the FBI man directly, "I have to concur with Dr. Majowski. This thing has been following an extremely steady orbit and it came out of nowhere. We don't have any other viable alternatives. Further, I think ..."

Just as Edward Simpson was preparing the *coup de grace* on his lowly FBI counterpart, the door again burst open, and in came rolling thunder: Brigadier General Margaret A. Menstrop, NASA liaison to the Joint Chiefs of Staff. All conversation stopped and the three men just stared.

She was a tiny woman, but anyone who knew her knew better than to underestimate her. Her face, like a sparrow's beak, was sharp and tapered into a pointed nose that grew nearly straight out from below deep-set black eyes. She perused the scene briefly then took a seat, sitting back and clasping her hands together in front of her.

"Now," she said calmly, "we can all stop the usual inter-office cluster-fuck and get a handle on this situation. First, next time you NASA folks deem it necessary to withhold information on large objects orbiting the Earth, there will certainly be new NASA folks. Second, this is a military matter. You two can stay" – she indicated Simpson and Kirby with a twitch of her eyes – "but do not feel free to expound on your ideas. Now let's get to it."

Dr. Majowski hesitated for a moment, wondering whether to continue, start over or simply dissolve, but before he could speak the door burst open again.

"It's coming down!" A wild eyed man screamed, "It's left its orbit and it's heading for L.A. like a bat out of hell."

"Shit," General Menstrop whispered, "Hand me that phone."

The shell of the ship glowed white-hot as it plowed through the dense atmosphere toward Belfin's target. Not far now, he thought, not far.

Eighty-eight-year-old Harvey Wilson, veteran of World War II ("the big one" as he called it), stood behind his shopping cart, on the corner of 4th and Wilshire wondering which way to walk. He'd been walking all day. Being homeless, jobless and generally everythingless, he wandered these streets every day. Somehow they still confused him. Suddenly he heard sirens start up in the distance; they did not sound like police sirens. To him they sounded more like the air-raid sirens he'd heard in the fifties and on the beach at Anzio. Ancient reflexes took over and Harvey looked up to the sky, waiting for the North Korean missiles to come streaking down and put humanity, or at least Santa Monica, out of its misery.

What he saw staggered him. He stood, shaking, riveted to the ground looking up into the bright sun and the huge black silhouette nearly blocking it out. What looked like a giant, burning building covered with projections of all shapes and sizes was coming down right in front of old Harvey. The air began to compress, and Harvey felt his knees buckle. Finally, moments before he was sure he would be crushed, the descending monolith stopped dead, hovering a scant 50 feet above the Penney's building on the corner of 3rd and Wilshire, emitting a high, keening whine. It extended four of what appeared to be feet, swiveled once, 180 degrees, then settled to the ground, destroying at least half of Penney's in the process and tearing a gouge in another building across the street. The noise abruptly stopped, leaving the metal carcass of the spaceship pinging and smoking, filling the air with an powerful ozone stench. Harvey did the only thing he could do. Just as he'd done when the door of the LCT opened at Anzio beach, he shit his pants and fainted dead away.

Zorgap trilled pleasure at Belfin's sure handling of the craft, seeing that they had settled to a soft and flawless landing on the primitive planet beneath. Belfin lifted his 50-ton bulk onto one massive pseudopod and headed toward the door. As she sensed him opening the hatch to the atmosphere of Earth, her hunger increased and her ravenous anticipation emanated in waves toward her mate. Belfin swiveled his preceptors briefly in her direction and with the Meldonian equivalent of a smirk, began to descend the ramp toward the center of Wilshire Boulevard.

Parkland Faraday had never seen action in Iraq, Afghanistan or even the seedier areas of Los Angeles. To say that his life was sheltered would have been an understatement, yet he found himself now, heading into the most incredible situation of his National Guard career. He was blond, of medium height and extremely pale. The men that served under him called him milquetoast, but Parkland Faraday had something none of them could match: Hugo Faraday for a father. Hugo had pushed his son hard as a child but was dismayed to find that young Parkland would be a failure at anything he tried. But Hugo could not accept that. And so, by pulling a few strings, moving a small trust account or two, and generally throwing his considerable weight around, Hugo had wangled his only son a commission in the National Guard. A few more pushes and phone calls over the years elevated young Parkland to the level of Colonel, serving as commander of the West Los Angeles battalion. And now it was Parkland, a Faraday, that rode atop a National Guard M-1A1 tank moving at high speed through parted traffic on Wilshire Boulevard. The wind blowing heroically – at least he fancied it that way – through his hair, he headed west toward an encounter for which no training could possibly prepare him: an encounter with a being from another planet.

Harvey Wilson got back to his feet, shivering in fear and feeling vague warmth and discomfort inside the three layers of his pants, just in time to see the immense alien descend from inside the flying building. It was fully 30 feet tall and looked like a huge pile of plastic mush, oozing forward on a snail's foot. Antennae bristled about its top and three huge stump-like arms waved to and fro in before it. On the front of the mass that Harvey thought might be its head, there were a set of purple lumps, resembling giant zits ready to burst and filled with gelatinous fluid. Harvey sat back down, immediately regretted the move and stared wide-eyed at the creature before him.

It began slowly crawling up the street, its antennae sweeping from side to side, crushing a red Honda Civic against the wall of a building as it moved past. A woman ran out of Crown Books just in front of the alien. Her eyes flew wide open and her shriek elevated to a shrill siren of fear. With an unexpected quickness, one of the creature's arms snapped out and grabbed the woman. Her shriek reached high C just as she was swept toward a set of slits across its mid-section. Harvey could see her struggling to no avail as the beast held her up to one slit then another. It stopped for a moment, holding the howling woman in front of it, apparently smelling her then expelled a great cloud of noxious fumes from the slits into the face of the woman. She fainted dead away and the alien tossed her aside like so much garbage. It continued on its way moving up the street, now swaying from side to side, devastating the walls and windows of the shops on either side of the street with swinging appendages.

Colonel Faraday, who now for the first time in his life actually felt like a soldier, did not have long to savor the feeling. As they topped a small rise and descended past 26th Street, he caught a glimpse of the immense spaceship straddling the road in front of him. His breath caught in his throat and he gasped for air. "Oh my God," he breathed.

He stood there, mouth agape, for nearly a full minute until a jolt of adrenaline hit his speeding heart. His voice returned a moment later and he shouted into his throat mike, "Prepare to fire as soon as we get close enough!" He could only hope someone would pay attention.

"Yes sir," came the terse reply, and all along the column of 12 M-1A1 tanks, the barrels swiveled up. Next to Parkland Faraday's tank, a half-track missile launcher matched their pace and its rack of rockets swiveled twice, then settled back into position. It too was ready to fire. Parkland took a deep breath, tried to blink, failed then ordered his men to sight on the alien now a mere 100 yards away. His tank halted just two feet from Harvey, who had not even noticed its approach. The others moved up to form a rough line around Parkland's lead tank, with the last four moving around to Arizona Street to try to flank the beast.

The alien seemed to move its head toward them briefly, sniffed, then returned to wreaking havoc on the cars and buildings before it. Its arms swung in perfect rhythm with its progress up the street, smashing first a 7-11 front window on one side, then a small deli on the other. Faraday gave the order to fire.

The air was filled with armor-piercing canister and shaped 120mm shells flying out to meet the alien and exploding in its hide. For a moment the creature seemed stunned after the first volley. Rising to an enormous height, it began plucking pieces of hot metal from its skin, smelling them briefly before tossing them aside. Hunkering back down, it turned suddenly to Anna Maria's Pizzeria on the south side of Wilshire. With one swing of its three massive appendages it swept the roof from the building, exposing the two panicked cooks, Anna Maria, and three huddling waitresses beneath.

Colonel Faraday saw it reaching inside the building and immediately ordered another volley of fire, this time joined by the other four tanks that had now moved up to catch the alien from behind. Now the full force of 16 tanks rapid-fired half of their payloads – over 68,000 kilos of armor-piercing and incendiary shells. They struck the alien all in a continuous barrage, creating a huge cloud of smoke that nearly engulfed the creature. It reared back, starting a slow retreat toward its ship. Faraday fairly beamed and ordered his men to open up in full, pelting the retreating alien with a barrage of high explosives and burning metal.

Five minutes later, the creature had withdrawn into its ship and Harvey Wilson had once again regained his feet, just in time to watch the ship soar into the sky and streak away. Squinting into the afternoon sun, he looked behind him and up at Parkland Faraday, who, his chest proud, was tracking the alien ship with his binoculars as it left the atmosphere. Harvey spat on the ground and muttered to himself something about kids and their play tanks.

Belfin's preceptors turned toward Zorgap, his antennae swinging wildly at the wondrous smell filling the cabin of their ship. Zorgap had once again become sulky. She snorted disdainfully toward him: "It still seems like a lot of trouble for a six pack and a pizza."

PART 3

THE TREASURE

Many, many years ago, high in a mountain range, there was a tiny kingdom known as the Northern Crag. The Northern Crag was a land of tall granite spires and lush green mountainsides. From these mountainsides more than 30 waterfalls fell into a deep cleft, at the bottom of which was a hidden valley cut down the middle by the rushing Cragfall River. All along the river were the clusters of thatch-roofed houses and buildings that made up the Kingdom itself. Beyond those small, but perfectly trimmed cottages, rich farmland reached to the very foot of the immense mountains that protected the valley. At the head of this valley, atop a small granite bench, sat a beautiful castle. Its walls were painted the purest white and each turret was crowned in emerald green. Its courtyard, the scene of the yearly harvest celebration, was paved in flagstones that seemed to change color as you walked over them. It was one of the most magnificent castles in the world, yet so remote that few except the townspeople ever looked upon it.

The king in this land was a wise and wonderful ruler, beloved and admired by his people. Above all, he was kind to his subjects. Often traveling the valley, he helped solve disputes, brought food and necessities to the poor and, most importantly, listened to the needs of his people. The Northern Crag was an idyllic place mainly due to his influence and caring.

As the years passed, the king grew old and one day found he could no longer move about the valley. Nonetheless, he continued to serve his people from his castle. During this time, it was said that the gates to the castle were never closed. He would accept visitors at any time, day or night, and he never feared for his safety. He continued to house the sick, feed the poor and expect little in return. Late one night, after hearing the needs of one caller after another, he retired to bed. He never awoke, having died peacefully in his sleep. When his servants found him in the morning there was a note, scrawled on a piece of parchment, clutched in his hand. Very soon there were heralds running through the streets, summoning everyone to the castle courtyard. The king, it seemed, had left a message for all his people to hear. At precisely one o'clock that afternoon, the king's crier stepped out onto the balcony overlooking the courtyard and asked for silence. "Loyal subjects of the Kingdom of the Northern Crag," he cried. "Your king ..." the crier paused, stricken with emotion, "has passed."

For a moment the crowd was dumbstruck and the crier looking down at them from his perch on the parapet could see the looks of confusion and sadness below. Their voices rose, some wailing, others talking loudly and the crier rang his bell once more for silence. The throng looked up as one, and waited. "The king has left a message for all his subjects," said the crier. "Please stand quietly and listen to your ruler's last words."

With that he cleared his throat, adjusted the small glasses perched on his nose and began to read. "My people, I have lived a long and rich life. As your king, I was blessed with a land of peace and plenty. All around you, the magnificence of what we have built together stands as a memorial to us all." At this the crowd began to mutter again, and the crier paused, waiting for silence to return. Moments later, with the people below quiet once more, he continued.

"I have, however, made a grievous mistake in that I never married. Thus, I leave you no heir to become your new king or queen. I realized this mistake years ago, but was too old and feeble to do anything about it, except ..." The crier looked up at the crowd now. A pin could be heard to drop in the silence below. "What I have done for you is perhaps better; only time will tell. And that thing is this: I have left behind a treasure. It is a treasure beyond counting, placed so that only the chosen may find it. Behind my castle lies a labyrinth of caves and passages. It is within these caverns that my treasure is hidden. He or she who finds it shall become your new ruler. You will know the true treasure by the note I have left with it. Find it, and my kingdom is yours. Strange as this may seem, I know that the person who finds it will be a fair and honest ruler.

But now my life fades and Valhalla waits. Farewell my people, I loved you all." With that the crier wiped his eyes and stepped down from the castle wall, simply walking away with no idea what to do next.

Word of the treasure soon spread to all the outlying areas. Men, women and even children tried their luck each day, wandering among the miles of endless tunnels and grottos. Some became lost, only to emerge days later, tired and hungry, while others simply went on, year after year, greedily determined to win the prize. Still more adventurers quietly gave up and went back to their lives. Time passed and no treasure was found. First months, then years, then more than a decade had gone by, and now only a handful of hopeful old men still made the trip into the caves hoping for a miracle. But no miracle came. Finally, the hunters were all but gone, and the treasure nearly forgotten.

Thirty years went by and still there was no king in the Northern Crag. It had been almost five years since anyone had even gone looking in the caves, and all hope was lost. In those 30 years, things had not gone well for the people of the valley. Without the king to feed them, the poor often went hungry. The castle fell into disrepair, and people began to leave the high valley to find their fortunes in the cities to the distant south. With no one to guide them and keep them together, the Northern Crag was falling apart.

In one village near the Cragfall, there lived a young boy named Edward who was the son of the shoemaker. Edward loved stories, and his father, having lived all of his 50 years in the valley, could re-tell every one. So each night, Edward would sit quietly by the fire in their small home and listen, while his father told tales of the old king. Often these stories would refer to the hidden treasure, so long sought for, but hopelessly lost. Sometimes the treasure was diamonds, sometimes gold and still other times silver, but it was always immense and its finder, of course, would rule the Northern Crag. Edward's imagination was fertile and though he was poor, he dreamed of one day finding the treasure himself. He would take care of things, he thought. He'd feed the poor he saw wandering in the streets. He'd make sure the sick kids got well and that everyone had a warm place to sleep. Yes, if he were king, things would be just as wonderful as they had been when his father was young! But alas he was too young, his father had said, to go hunting in dark caves for a mythical trove.

But eventually young Edward grew up and one bright sunny day, decided it was time to venture inside the caves. After a few hours he discovered, as many had before him, a small room, just off the main tunnel. When it had first been located, it was learned that the king as a child had played in this room. The mementos of a child-king were untouched and still there, though dusty with age, out of respect for his memory. Within sat a comfortable upholstered chair, next to a tiny hearth festooned with colorful animals painted on the mantle. Beside the chair there was a reading table and a small shelf of books that the king had owned when he was a child. There was a stool to set one's feet upon while in the chair, and next to that sat a small pine toy-box. A bit sheepishly, Edward slid carefully into the chair and imagined himself a young king in his own private world, hidden away from the township outside. He tried to envision what the king might have thought, sitting in this warm, cheery hideaway, when his eyes were drawn again to the toy-box.

Now Edward was not so far beyond the years of a child, and he was intrigued to see what a king might play with. Leaning forward, he drew the chest to his feet and lifted the lid. Inside, there were exquisite toys of all descriptions. There were wooden soldiers brightly painted in red and blue, little dolls with floppy arms and eyes made of shining buttons, toy carts and horses and building blocks with pictures of animals painted on them. What caught his eye and held it however, was an old and worn stuffed puppy. As Edward gently lifted the ragged toy in his hands, he felt a rush of warmth in his heart as he thought of his own stuffed bear, Willie, lost forever in some cubbyhole at home. He noticed that one ear was nearly off, and that the entire body of once lush fur was now no more than a rag. Somehow though, it felt good in his hands and fitting that he hold it. This puppy, like his bear Willie, was the beloved toy of a little boy long gone. Closing his eyes, he held it to his chest, feeling comfort emanate from the tiny body in his arms. As he leaned back, he cuddled the puppy even closer, but as he did it, he heard a small crackling sound.

For a moment he thought he'd torn the damaged ear, but upon looking the puppy over he could find no sign of damage. The ear still held desperately on and the body was intact. Examining the puppy further, he found a small tear in the back, or was it more of a pocket? Pulling the sides of the tear apart, he found a faded piece of wrinkled parchment inside. On it was the King's seal and a note that read:

"You who have found this must truly know the value of things most dear. The puppy you hold in your hands was my childhood friend and the one thing in the world I cherished most. It was my treasure, though I'm sure it is not what you expected. As I write this, I notice that it is much the worse for wear, but I hope you can see through the grime and wear, and find in it the love that it meant for a small boy growing up to be King. When I was alone, Puppy was there to comfort me. When I heard thunder, Puppy snuggled dose and whispered that it was only a storm. Puppy taught me to love and to give to others as he gave to me. I think anyone who knows and values a toy like this in their life, knows how to love those around them. You will be a fine ruler someday. Take my Puppy with you now for good luck, as it always gave me, and greet your new Kingdom, for you have found the treasure of the Northern Crag."

A CAVE IN TEMESCAL CANYON

I'm going in. You coming or not?" Jimmy Nolan looked at his best friend in annoyance. Shelby Phillips, small and stick-thin, stood motionless, his unruly red hair shifting in the afternoon wind. He was frightened and could not bring his eyes up to meet Jimmy's. The two had just climbed up among some rocks along the ridge bordering the Temescal Canyon Hiking Trail. Each had hiked here for years, first with their parents and later with each other, pretending to be commandos, cowboys, or even Indians. The week before, as they'd been exploring up the sides of the canyon, Shelby had found the opening to a small cave. At first it did not look like much, but as the boys examined it, they found it went deep into the side of the canyon wall. It had been late that afternoon and they'd had to leave before they could go much further in than the immediate opening. On the way home, with the early evening summer sun still strong in the sky, they had decided to keep the location and even the existence of "their cave" a secret. Especially from their respective, repulsive older brothers. Now, after a week of quiet talk and secretive glances over lunch at school, they had returned. It was early Saturday morning on a July day that promised to be magnificent, and they were not expected home for hours.

Jimmy was dressed in his habitual blue jeans and white T-shirt, of which very little white remained. Shelby, with his painfully pale legs protruding from baggy shorts, wore a black T-shirt that said AC-DC on the front. He did not know who AC-DC was, but his dad thought the shirt was cool, so he wore it every chance he got. Each had a flashlight.

The climb up the side of the Canyon had left both winded and dirty, but excited at the same time. At 11 years old, Jimmy was big for his age. His dirty brown hair was cut short like his sports heroes wore theirs. His olive complexion made the sun easy on him, while Shelby suffered sunburn all summer long from playing outside with Jimmy. He never seemed to care though; at 11, with an adventurous friend like Jimmy, there was no time to be bothered with sunburns. They looked at each other now, and Shelby sighed deeply, then led the way inside.

The opening was large enough for them to walk upright inside and, once they trained their flashlights on the back wall of the cave, they could see a crease that led much deeper into the earth than they imagined. "Man this is awesome, dude ... can you believe this?" Shelby exclaimed.

"Yeah ... it's amazing how deep this goes. Let's see what's back further." Jimmy brushed past Shelby before the smaller boy could protest and slid in behind the crease.

"Hey, wait up, Jimbo." Shelby moved into the crease now himself and found it was much wider than it looked. A passage led deeper in the recesses of the cave and Shelby shone his flash upwards. Tiny mineral deposits reflected his light and, fascinated by the sparkling crystals overhead, he ran smack into Jimmy who'd stopped dead just ahead of him.

"Shhhhh..." Jimmy's whisper was urgent.

"Wha..."

"*Shhhhhhhhh*!! There's something back there man, shut up!" Jimmy hissed.

Cautiously, Shelby peered over his friend's shoulder as Jimmy slowly moved his light around the back of the cave. The cave opened wider here, into a small room about 30 feet deep and 20 feet wide. As Jimmy's flashlight beam explored the area, Shelby saw nothing other than a large brown rock in the middle of the room, and more of the shining minerals.

"There is nothing back here, man," Shelby whispered.

"I heard it Shel, I swear I did. Something was moving around, shuffling and making a kind of snorting noise ... real softly."

"Well, whatever it was is gone now. There's nothing here but that ro..." Shelby could not finish his sentence because as he spoke, the rock moved.

Jimmy started to back away, his eyes wide with fright and pushing Shelby behind him, as the rock rose up onto four distinct but stubby legs. Just as Jimmy's shaking flashlight beam rose to the creature's back, it turned its head toward them from in front. The light reflected from a set of long, sharp white teeth and a pair of luminous green eyes. That was enough for Jimmy and Shelby: they both turned and ran from the cave as fast as their feet would carry them. "Hurry up, hurry up, hurry up!" cried Jimmy, shoving Shelby in front of him like a running back pushing a blocker.

"I'm goin' man, I'm goin'... holy smokes what was that!?" Shelby panted just as he passed through the opening of the cave into the sunlight.

"I dunno but it had some serious teeth."

Once outside, the boys scrambled down a small dirt slide and into some bushes at the base of the cave. They landed together and turned simultaneously to look back at the opening. Their hearts beating syncopated drumbeats inside their heaving chests, the two lay mesmerized, staring at the cave, sure that death would emerge at any moment.

"Let's go Jim, let's go home," Shelby felt like he was going to begin sobbing, but he held fast against losing face with his friend.

"Just a minute Shel. It's not coming out ... wonder what that means?"

"I don't care man, that was some kind of mountain lion or something, and we shouldn't be messing with it."

"No it's not Shel. It looked like a rock, remember? If it was a mountain lion, it would have had fur. It's something different, but I can't figure out what."

"Well who the heck cares what it is, it's got big monster teeth and I don't want to meet up with it again! No sir, not one bit I don't!"

"Shhhh..." Jimmy grasped his friend's arm, "you hear that?"

"What? No Jimmy, I don't..."

"*Shhhh*! Man, can't you shut up? Just listen for a minute."

Shelby looked at Jimmy's face for a moment, saw the exasperation there and sighed deeply. "Alright ..." They listened. For a moment there was nothing, then a distinct but quiet sound issued from inside the cave. It sounded like ...

"Sobbing ... it sounds like a little kid crying, Shel. That thing is crying!"

"Or there's some little kid in there it's about to eat up, and *he's* crying! I think I might have heard that mountain lions can make a sound like that ... Come on Jimbo, let's ..."

"Shhhh. Listen, that's not a kid getting eaten, that's someone crying. Whatever that thing is, it's scared to death, man. Let's go take another look."

"Uh uh, no way, man, I am *not* going back in there." Shelby shook his head fiercely.

Jimmy turned to him, bright blue eyes peering out of a dirty brown face. "Okay Shel, look, you stay here. I'm just going to slide up there and peek inside. If I start yelling, you start yelling too and go running for some help."

"Jimmy I don't think it's a very good idea ..." but it was too late. Jimmy had already scurried up to the cave opening. He looked back once, held his finger up to his lips to signal for quiet, then slipped inside.

"Ohhhh maaan, this is baaad, I just know it," Shelby whispered to himself.

After a few tense minutes, Shelby thought he heard something from inside the cave. It sounded like voices. "A kid in a monster suit ... that's what it must be, some kid," he thought. He listened more closely, now able to make out Jimmy's voice and another, higher-pitched voice. The other sounded like a smaller child, hard to tell boy or girl, but definitely a smaller kid. Shelby rose to his knees and moved up the slope to hear better.

The voices continued, speaking in soft tones. He could hear Jimmy's voice more distinctly and it seemed serene, almost as if Jimmy were trying to calm the kid down. Shelby moved further up the slope to within 10 feet of the opening. He could hear more now, but could still not make out the words. The situation seemed clear enough though, and finally, his curiosity winning out over fright and caution, Shelby stood and climbed the last few feet up to the cave mouth. Just as he looked inside, a pair of shining eyes burst from the cave right at him.

"Whaaaa!!!" Shelby roared in terror, and started to turn. A hand grabbed his elbow and spun him back around.

"Slow down dude, your gonna kill yourself!" Jimmy spoke calmly, holding his friend.

"Man, you scared me out of my pants there ... why didn't you make some noise when you were coming out, let me know, you know!" Shelby's voice was still shaking.

"You gotta see this, come on," Jimmy spun on his heel and headed back into the cave.

Shelby took a deep breath and calmed himself. "You're gonna regret this Shel old buddy," he said to the sky, then switched on his flashlight and walked inside.

Jimmy was waiting for him at the crease, his flashlight beam aimed at the ground. "He's scared, so don't make any sudden moves. It might be dangerous or something. But you have *got* to see this, you won't believe it man, you just won't believe it." Jimmy started around the crease when Shelby grabbed him and pulled him back.

"Exactly *who* is scared, Jimbo, and why would it be dangerous? What the heck is going on?"

Jimmy held his own light up to his face and grinned at his friend. "Just come on, you sincerely won't believe this one. It's one for the books I tell ya, now come on!"

Shelby followed Jimmy cautiously into the depths of the cave. The rounded the last turn and now faced the small room. Shelby's mouth formed an "O" and his eyes went wide as he shone his light inside. The room was the same, but the rock had moved.

And it was no longer a rock.

What had seemed to be brownish in color, now sparkled in the beam of Jimmy's flashlight as hard greenish scales. Four stubby legs supported the beast and when the head swiveled around to look at the two boys, its tail unraveled from beneath and swept out behind. Thin tendrils of smoke rose from the creature's snout as it watched them warily. Slowly, almost timidly, it turned toward them. There was no mistaking the mythical reptile before them. And although it was smallish, not quite rising to the boys' waistlines, it was most definitely a dragon. Neither Shelby nor Jimmy could move.

"Uh ... hello?" A child-like voice somehow found its way around razor sharp fangs.

"Oh man, Jimmy, it's talking to us!" Shelby croaked.

"Hi," Jimmy said, as if he were talking to another kid he'd just met on the playground.

"I'm sorry if I scared you. I'm not really used to people," The young dragon's voice sounded misty, as if it were about to cry.

"Was that you we heard outside?" Jimmy asked.

The dragon sniffed, causing smoke to be drawn back into its nostrils, "Yes ... I'm afraid so."

As the boys watched a crystalline tear issued from one saucer sized eye and slid over the scales of its nose. "Why are you crying? Are you hurt?" Shelby had finally found his voice.

"No," the dragon said, its voice wavering.

"What's wrong then?" Jimmy asked, taking a step forward and kneeling so that his face was even with the dragon's.

"I seem to have gotten myself lost," the dragon replied, sniffling again and holding back tears with great effort.

"Well ... hm, maybe we can help you. Where do you live?" Jimmy asked.

"Where does he live? What's the heck's wrong with you, Jimbo, Where does he live? You gotta be kidding. He's a fairytale, for goodness sake!"

Jimmy glared at his friend for a moment then returned his gaze to the dragon.

"I'm not from around here – your world, that is. I think I live in another one. It's much nicer than this one ... greener at least. Anyway, I think something happened and I slipped into this world. There aren't any knights around are there? My mom says knights are real bad."

"No knights, dragon ... hey, what do we call you anyway? Do you have a name?"

"Yeah," the dragon sniffed. "I'm called Smaug."

"Well then. I'm Jimmy, and this is my friend Shelby. Pleased to meet you Smaug." Jimmy smiled briefly holding out his hand, then retracting it. The dragon seemed to calm slightly.

"How can we help you find your way back? I don't think either of us has any experience with this sort of thing, but we can try at least." Shelby also took a step forward now, his curiosity now having fully overcome his fear.

"I don't know!" This seemed to upset the dragon, and its body shook as it sobbed for a full minute.

"Listen, calm down now, Smaug. We'll figure something out. First though, are you okay, are you hurt, hungry, anything like that?" Jimmy edged closer.

"Yeah ... I'm hungry. I'm not hurt ... I'm just scared and little hungry, that's all."

Shelby and Jimmy exchanged glances. "Shelby? What do you suppose we can feed to a dragon?"

"Well," Shelby's face took on a look of hard concentration, "I don't think we have any fair maidens handy."

Jimmy smiled, then turned back to the dragon. "What do you eat anyway? Maybe we can get you something."

"Well, my mom and I eat a lot of pigs and goats – you know, farm animals, that sort of thing. I'm not old enough yet to kill anything, but my mom brings me stuff. All cooked and everything."

"Cooked?" Jimmy's eyebrows raised. "Does that mean what I think it means?"

The dragon showed white fangs in what appeared to be a smile. "Oh yeah. Nice hot fire-breath; works very nicely."

"Can you do that? Breathe fire, I mean?" It was Shelby's turn to advance now, and he stood only about a foot from the dragon.

"A little. Not much yet, but it's coming. I'm just a little smoker now, but give me a few centuries and watch out!" Smaug's face looked proud now, his tears all but gone.

"Centuries?"

"Yeah. We dragons live for an awfully long time. I'm not really sure how long. I've never seen one of us die, but then again, there aren't many of us left, even in my world." The dragon's eyes were downcast again, as if he were thinking. Finally he looked up. "Do you have any meat at all? I'd eat just about anything right now."

Shelby looked over at Jimmy who simply shrugged. "Listen, we don't go carrying meat around with us ... but you know, I think we could get something for you. Will you stay here?"

The dragon looked around the cave for a moment. "Nowhere else to go. My mom told me that if I ever slipped, uh, fell through a crack into another world that is, that I should just stay put. So I guess that's what I'll do."

"Okay, look, Shelby and I will go get you something and bring it back. You keep your chin up in the meantime. It won't take long, okay?"

Smaug looked at them with mournful eyes and nodded. With an effort, he again folded his tail around his legs and knelt into what appeared to be greenish lump. "Hurry back," he said over his shoulder and the boys could hear the moisture in his voice.

"We will. Don't worry, we'll be back in a flash." Jimmy looked over at Shelby. "Let's go man. You guys have that freezer full of meat. We can take a bunch and your dad'll never know."

The boys exited the cave in a rush, babbling the entire way home and scarcely slowing from a dead run. As they reached Shelby's house, the two pulled up short and quickly ran to the side of the house.

"Is that your brother's bike, man?"

"Yeah, his and Chip's and Roger's too. They're all here, Jimbo, the whole bunch."

"We can't let them in on this, Shel, promise me. This dragon's ours. If they hear about this, they'll do something bad, I just know it."

"No argument there." Shelby looked at his friend, his brow furrowed in thought. "Listen Jim, here's what we'll do. We'll just slip out to the garage, grab a bunch of steaks and stuff, and off we go out the back. Got it?"

"Sounds good, Shel. Let's do it!"

With nothing more said, the two boys stood, brushed themselves off, crept carefully past the house and into the garage. In moments they had filled a grocery bag with steak, ground beef and roasts from the enormous store of meat in the garage freezer.

"By the time we get there this stuff will have begun to thaw, but mostly it's still gonna be frozen. You think that'll be a problem for Smaug?" Jimmy commented as they walked across in front of the house, heading for Temescal Canyon.

"You know, Jimbo, somehow I don't think that's going to be much problem for a dragon." Shelby smiled and Jimmy started giggling. They broke into a trot with one quick glance over their shoulders, and headed down the street.

In the front window of the house, three heads watched the two small boys leave with the brown paper bag. "Something's up with those guys, Kev. They've got some big bag of something with them, and it looks like your brother's got a flashlight."

"Um hm. I've got an idea we ought to follow those two. You know, make sure they don't get into trouble." Kevin smiled at his two friends and they smirked back.

"Let's go," Chip said in his best commando voice.

In just under 20 minutes, Shelby and Jimmy, both breathless, arrived at the cave entrance. Without hesitation Shelby clicked on his flashlight and they plunged inside. A short distance behind them, Kevin, Roger and Chip huddled near a small clump of scrub sage. Kevin squinted into the sun.

"A cave, guys! Looks like they found a cave ... interesting." The other two sat silent, waiting for Kevin to take the lead.

"Smaug? You there?" Shelby called out, not wanting to startle a potentially dangerous young dragon.

"Yeah, still here, guys. Hey, something smells good!"

"Beef!" Jimmy cried triumphantly holding up the bag, "and plenty of it!"

"That's so nice of you, guys." The dragon's eyes seemed wary. "People are a strange lot. At least that's what my mom says. But you guys seem okay." The dragon ended brightly.

"Okay, well, here you go. Shel, help me unwrap this stuff, will ya?"

Suddenly a blinding light filled the cave. The boys stiffened, then turned to squint into three brilliant flashlights held by the older boys. Instantly they dropped the meat and the dragon shriveled into a whimpering ball.

"So, what do we have here, guys? What you guys got there, eh? Some kind of animal?"

"I'm not an animal," came a softly muffled reply.

"It speaks? Is that your other buddy Remy in a costume or something? What's going on here Shelby, what the heck do you guys think you are up to?" Kevin stepped forward, a seemingly huge shadow behind the flashlight.

"It's ... it's ... it's a ... a um uh," Shelby's mouth would not form the words.

"It's a dragon, Kevin. A baby one. We found it and it's ours!" Jimmy stood up now, ready to face down the older boys. The three older boys started first to chuckle, then laughed out loud, holding their sides and choking for breath. It was Roger who regained his composure first.

"A dragon? You guys want us to believe you found a dragon? Now that's a new one."

"It is a dragon and it is ours!" Jimmy shouted stubbornly.

As the boys were talking, the dragon had slowly allowed its curiosity to overcome its fear, and had arisen and turned to face the boys. It poked its snout out from between where Shelby and Jimmy stood and looked into the light held by the newcomers.

"Could you turn off that light? It's really bright," Smaug said softly.

The older boys were suddenly dumbstruck. They stared at the tableau in front of them, two small boys and one small dragon's head poking out from in between.

"Ha ma ha ma ha ma ha," was all Roger could utter.

"It's a ... it's a ... it's a..." Chip stammered.

"Dragon!" Kevin completed, somehow finding his voice.

For a moment all five boys simply stood there. None knew what to say. The dragon finally spoke again, more clearly this time.

"The lights, fellas? Can you turn them off or point them somewhere else?"

"This is a real dragon, guys," Kevin finally said, almost preternaturally calm. "A real one and there aren't any such things as dragons. You guys know what that means?" The others didn't answer, but turned to Shelby's older brother. "It means were gonna be *rich*!" his voice rose to a crescendo. "Rich, I tell you, rich. This dragon of ours, we're gonna sell it to a zoo or a circus or something. We're gonna make a mint. We'll be on TV!!"

Jimmy frowned, then faced again to the older boys. "Now wait just a minute here. This is *our* dragon not yours. And he's not going in some zoo. He's a nice guy and we can't sell him. What's wrong with you, Kevin, are you some kind of ..." Jimmy never finished. In a flash Kevin stepped forward, bringing his face close to his smaller brother's.

"Now you listen here ..." Kevin began.

Shelby began backing away, the dragon moving with him, steadily toward the rear of the cave.

Kevin looked at Roger first, then at Chip. He smiled a self-satisfied grin and that was returned by the others. They readied themselves to move in and grab the dragon, but something stopped them. Neither of the young boys, a moment ago trying bravely to face them down, nor the dragon, were any longer looking at them. Kevin's eyes moved from one to the other. All three had the same wide-eyed look of absolute terror on their faces, and were staring straight over his shoulder. Suddenly Roger and Chip were no longer next to him. Those two were uttering whimpering noises and backing toward the walls of the cave, their eyes bugging out. Slowly, Kevin turned. Behind him was another dragon, and while he could only see the face, it was clear that this one was fully-grown.

At that moment, Kevin the tough, Kevin the brave, Kevin the strong melted into abject horror and did something he hadn't done since he was four years old. He peed his pants. From behind him came a tiny timid voice.

"Mom?" the baby dragon croaked.

The massive head surveyed the boys, snorted a thin jet of fire, then withdrew. The little dragon hurriedly began to follow. Just as it was about to exit, the small reptile turned and seemed to smile once more at Shelby and Jimmy. "It's my mom, guys. I have to go now. It was nice meeting you, Jimmy and Shelby. I don't know you other guys' names, but you should be nicer to these little ones. Anyway, I gotta run, but here's something to remember me by."

With that Smaug shook himself and one shimmering scale fell too the floor of the cave. The dragon winked and started to turn. It was Kevin who reacted first, practically diving for the scale, his gleeful face full of satisfaction. But just as his hand reached for it, a clawed foot came down hard, covering it and nearly crushing his hand. "Tsk tsk tsk young human. This is for the nice ones. You leave it alone. Or ..." The dragon never finished. It simply lifted its foot and jetted a satisfying burst of steam into the room. Kevin backed off and watched as Shelby came forward and picked up the scale. Suddenly the dragon was gone.

Moments later the boys emerged, blinking, into the sun. Overhead they caught the barest glimpse of two shapes folding into the clouds, one small, one large; and then they were gone.

A DOG'S TALE

It feels so good to be curled up on Dougie's bed. In fact, as we get older, Dougie and I, I think we enjoy sleeping more and more. I've heard Dougie say to his friends "That's my dog Rocket," as if I belonged to him instead of the other way around. I guess it's okay if he thinks he's in charge. If it makes him happy, well, that's all the more petting and ball playing for me, so I can't really complain. If Dougie only knew. And puppy, did he ever come close that day.

I wish I'd slept in that day like I am doing today, but it wasn't summer yet and Dougie was heading off for school. Of course I could have just stayed inside the fence and sacked out on the lawn all day, but after a few hours I was getting restless. Things might have turned out differently if I'd done that, and maybe not so well and I certainly would have missed a pretty grand adventure. I guess I should tell you first that I'm a cocker spaniel. Well sort of anyway. I'm not really sure, but I do kind of look like one. I'm all black, with short legs and a little white splotch on my chest fur. I have big dark eyes (very effective for obtaining the odd head pat or chin scratch), and I don't slobber. Not like those stupid pugs next door, but then, without them ...

As I was saying, that day started out like most. The sun was out and I watched through the slats in the fence as Dougie and his mother got in their car and drove off for school. Now I've taught Dougie all kinds of tricks. For example, he can throw the ball for me (half the time I make *him* fetch it!), he can rub my tummy just like I like it and he'll chase me around anytime I want. So I don't really understand why he has to go to school, but it does give me some free time. But I digress.

After some sleeping, I was feeling pretty frisky that day. Must have been the new kibbles, or that extra piece of bacon that Dougie snuck me under the table. So as soon as I felt the urge, I gave that loose slat in the fence a little push and went out into the front yard. The first order of business was going around and giving everything a good sniff, making sure to pee in every other bush. In moments I heard a familiar snuffling, snorking sound behind me. Turning, I was greeted by two of the ugliest creatures on earth, *and* two of my best friends, the pugs. Their names are Harmony and Monte (Harmony is Monte's mom) and the two of them are inseparable. We greeted each other in the normal way; a few butt sniffs, a face lick or two and then we all resumed sniffing and peeing. Our routine was disturbed when a small red car pulled up in front of my house. For a bare instant, I felt that heart surge that happens every time Dougie comes home, but I realized that it wasn't him when a blond haired youth got out and started yelling across the street for someone named Darlene to come out. He got no reply and, leaving the car running, jogged across the street and into the large white house there.

The pugs and I found this episode insufficiently entertaining and so headed off to explore the neighborhood. With the pugs, you don't have to say much. They just sort of follow along and go wherever you go. You always know they are there because of those bizarre sounds they make. I don't think those snouts they have are designed for breathing, but again, I digress. We had just rounded the corner from our street onto the next when we saw him for the first time.

"A puppy," snorted Monte derisively, though he was mostly puppy himself.

"Stupid puppy," echoed Harmony.

I looked the newcomer over. He was a cute little fella; a beagle by the look of him, brown and white and all floppy and clumsy, stepping on his ears and sniffing around the neighbor's trashcans. He didn't appear to notice us so I decided to go over and say hello. Just as I was about to step into the street, I stopped dead in my tracks. Of course this caused both pugs to ram into my butt and nearly shove me out into traffic, but, with some effort, I held my ground. Out of the house had come a little girl. She could not have been much more than six years old, wearing a pair of white feet-pajamas with tiny pink elephants on them. She trotted in that half-stumble humans call running, scooped up the puppy into her arms and gave him a big squeeze. It reminded me of how Dougie used to hold me and my nose got all cold and wet thinking about it. I was smiling my best doggy smile and watching, when I heard a shrill human voice.

"Connie Jo! Connie Jo, where are you?" The girl's mother stepped out of the front of the house calling her name. From where she stood, her mother could not see Connie Jo, nor did she notice when Connie Jo looked over her shoulder to where her mother's voice was coming from and accidentally dropped the puppy into one of the trash cans. The little girl looked confused for a moment, but one more "Connie Jo!" from her mother, this one at an even higher pitch, and she ran into the back door of the house, shutting it behind her. Connie Jo's mom looked around for a second or two, then turned back toward the house. Then I heard her say "Oh there you are young lady, where'd you ..." The door shut and I could hear no more. I looked at the pugs, they looked at me and we all looked over at the trashcan, which was now wobbling frantically as one very frightened puppy thrashed around inside.

"Trash can," Harmony said simply.

"Trash can," Monte added.

"We'll have to knock it over," I said and we all started across the street.

I live with an older dog named Bunny (she hates that name, and who can blame her!) and she taught me long ago about the street. Cars are on the street and while they may look fun, they are big, hard and can make lunch meat out of you in the sniff of a nose. So I don't just run out there like those stupid pugs and this time was no exception. Just as they started off the curb, I looked up the road and sure enough a huge blue truck came rolling down towards us.

"Pugs!" I barked, "Car coming! Get your curlicue-tailed butts back on this curb!" The pugs looked at me stupidly, then each other, then came back over and started sniffing the grass as if nothing had happened.

It turned out this was no ordinary truck, it was the trash truck. Before we could do anything the cans were scooped up, one by one and emptied into the back of the blue truck, puppy and all. I was frozen in place. The pugs continued snuffling and sniffing, not seeming to notice anything amiss.

Now I've been outside when these blue trucks show up many times. When the back of the truck gets full, the giant humans pull this lever and this terrible sounds starts. The blue truck then eats the stuff in its back end. This big blue truck was about to have its first taste of fresh puppy. The men jumped on the truck and it turned the corner and headed down the street. I knew I had to think fast or it was all over for our new neighbor – but how to get to him before they pulled that lever? Heck, how could we catch them at all?! As the sound of the trash truck faded, I became aware of another sound behind me. The blond youth's car ... still running. I looked at the pugs and they looked back at me.

For once in their little sniffing, snorking, slobbering lives, I saw some intelligence flash behind those bug eyes of theirs. "Pugs! Follow me!" I barked. I ran to the side of the red car and stood sideways. It was our luck that day that the car's window was open.

"Harmony, go!" I didn't need to tell her any more than that. She leapt up onto my back and bounded into the car. Monte was right behind without even so much as a snarl from me. The pugs were in and I was right behind. "On the floor, pugs. Harmony, take that right pedal and put your paws on it. Monte, the left pedal. Hurry!" I panted.

I bit down on the shift lever, and moved it the way I'd seen Dougie's dad do it a thousand times. Click-click-click and the car started moving. Once I felt it surge, I stood on my hind legs, put both paws on the wheel – 10 o'clock and two o'clock – and growled to Harmony, "Punch it, old girl!" The car leapt beneath me as Harmony bore down and we headed up the street following the blue truck.

The Singleton's had not put out their trash, nor had the Konelton's, so the blue truck sped past both their houses with our red car furiously in pursuit. That's when I read the sign on the back of the trash truck. The one that says "Beware! This vehicle makes sudden stops." I hadn't thought of that. In moments, it stopped dead and we were careening toward it with a vengeance. I realized then that I hadn't told Harmony to back off the gas and we were still accelerating!

"Harmony, let go! Monte, *now*!" I barked.

I only had a moment to see those giant humans jumping out of the way frantically as we slid into the back of that trash truck, before we were all three thrown forward and knocked silly. It took me a moment to get my wits but I quickly jumped out the window onto the ground, ran past the stunned humans and jumped into the back of the truck. Despite the fact that there were some of the most amazing and wonderful smells in that truck I can ever remember, it took me only an instant to locate one shivering and frightened puppy and pull him free. I carried the little fella by the scruff of the neck (just like our mommas used to carry us) out of the truck and set him on the ground. He grinned at me sheepishly and licked my face. I grinned back, returned his lick and then started to relax, when it hit me. I'd forgotten all about the pugs!

Of course I needn't have worried. The pugs were both on their backs getting belly rubs from the astonished and laughing giants. I accepted a head pat, then gave a quick authoritative bark and headed my charges back down the road. It wouldn't be long before that puppy was missed and we had to get him home. It took the pugs a minute or two to get the picture, but soon we were all padding down the sidewalk, a happy foursome forgetting what had happened. Even the blond youth running past us yelling "My car! My car!" didn't faze us. We'd saved the day and were enjoying the green grass along the sidewalk, marking some new territory and generally smelling our freedom.

The smell didn't last long though. Just as we were about to pass the Konelton's I noticed something else in the air. The pugs smelled it too, and I could hear them snuffling behind me. It was not a good smell. In fact, it was a very bad smell. The smell of bulldog. One Samuel Jackson Bulldog in particular – the meanest, nastiest dog on the block. Not someone to mess with. I quickly looked to the side where his fence gate was and to my horror it stood open. A moment later he stepped out of the bushes and stood before us blocking our path.

"Hmmm ... what have we here?" he snarled. "Rocket, I see you're still hanging around with the intellectual elite. And you dear pugs ... bite-sized little pugs ... don't you look scrumptious today."

"Leave us alone, Sam," I snarled back, but I was backing up all the same and running into the pugs, also backpedaling. Eventually we bunched up into a shivering mass of dog.

Suddenly I felt the puppy sliding under me and his head emerged from between my front paws. He saw the bulldog and started barking up a storm.

"Oh, even better ... puppy ... food!" Samuel growled.

The puppy became frantic and his yapping rose to a fever pitch. I pushed my chin down onto his head and tried to comfort him, but I could feel something wet and warm on my feet. Darned puppy was peeing himself ... or was that me?! Samuel Jackson bulldog took a step forward, and that's when it happened. We all heard it. There is no sound like it in the world, and no dog can resist it. We all, including Samuel Jackson, turned our heads, lost all thought of the fight and started wagging as hard as dogs can wag. It was the carpool pulling up next door.

Samuel's Allison was first out of the car, then my Dougie, then the pugs' boy Bradley and finally a new kid we hadn't seen before. There is no joy in this world like the joy you feel when your boy or girl comes home. We ran to them and leapt up (yes, even mean ol' Samuel) to get our greeting. The new kid picked up the puppy and gave him a hug, "What're you doing out here?" he asked, before turning to walk home. It occurred to me that I should tell him, but thought better of it. I was in my Dougie's arms and there is no place on earth like that.

www.ingramcontent.com/pod-product-compliance
Lightning Source LLC
Chambersburg PA
CBHW030814310726
48980CB00006B/488/J
* 9 7 8 0 6 1 5 8 1 7 6 4 4 *